Fire

San Juan Shadows - Book 1

San Juan Shadows - Book 1

Lynnette BONNER

FIRE
SAN JUAN SHADOWS, Book 1

Published by Serene Lake Publishing
Copyright © 2018 by Lynnette Bonner. All rights reserved.

Cover design by Lynnette Bonner of Indie Cover Design, images ©
  www.peopleimages.com, File: # ID 442185
  www.depositphotos.com, File: #4940220
Book design by Jon Stewart of Stewart Design

Scriptures taken from the Holy Bible, New International Version®, NIV®. Copyright © 1973, 1978, 1984, 2011 by Biblica, Inc.™ Used by permission of Zondervan. All rights reserved worldwide. www.zondervan.com The "NIV" and "New International Version" are trademarks registered in the United States Patent and Trademark Office by Biblica, Inc.™

ISBN: ISBN: 978-1-942982-11-1

Fire is a work of fiction. References to real people, events, establishments, organizations, or locales are intended only to provide a sense of authenticity and are used fictitiously. All other characters, incidents, and dialogue are drawn from the author's imagination.

OTHER CONTEMPORARY BOOKS BY LYNNETTE BONNER

THE PACIFIC SHORES SERIES
Contemporary Romance

Beyond the Waves - BOOK ONE
Caught in the Current - BOOK TWO
Song of the Surf - BOOK THREE
Written in the Sand - BOOK FOUR

THE ISLANDS OF INTRIGUE SERIES
Contemporary Romantic Suspense

The Unrelenting Tide - BOOK ONE
(There are more books in this series by other authors.)

THE RIVERSONG SERIES
Contemporary Romance

Angel Kisses and Riversong - BOOK ONE
Soft Kisses and Birdsong - BOOK TWO

Find all other books by Lynnette Bonner at:
www.lynnettebonner.com

Chapter 1

The flame of the Bunsen burner flickered blue and white beneath the bubbling beaker of orange viscous liquid.

A sniff indicated that the mixture seemed just right this time. A little stronger than the last batch.

Satisfaction spread. This was going to bring to life the dreams of a nice house, a fancy car, and maybe even an offshore account.

Kids were going to eat this stuff up like pigs in slop.

An almost imperceptible smirk tugged at lips that had essentially forgotten how to smile in the last few years.

Pigs in slop was an apt description for high schoolers these days. If kids had more self-control they wouldn't be susceptible to temptations such as this. In fact, maybe exposure to this would do them a favor. One trip on the hallucinogenic ride of this drug might scare some of them straight. But hopefully not too many.

The smirk faded a bit.

Too bad some kids had died after taking that last batch. Hopefully, the smaller doses that would be recommended with this batch would prevent more deaths. After all, killing off all the clientele wasn't such a great business model.

On the other hand... It was a little bit like helping out nature. Survival of the fittest and all. Those who were meant to live, would. And those who weren't, well, wouldn't.

"Just doing my part." The murmur was too loud in the

echoing stillness of the empty chemistry classroom and caused a jolt of anxiety. This time of night, no one else was likely in the school. Still, it was time to get out of here. Wouldn't want one of the teachers showing up and asking questions.

A check of the thermometer showed that the liquid had reached the right temperature. Perfect timing.

A nitrile heat-resistant glove protected the hand that lifted the beaker and poured the contents onto the cooling tray. Immediately, the substance began to crackle, forming perfect little crystalline fragments that glowed like red hot coals in the hand-sheltered beam of the cell phone flashlight. The creation was perfect. Now it just needed a name. So far sales had been pushed with "try a new drug in beta and tell me what you think." But with this new phase it was time to up the marketing.

"Fire." The word tumbled out with barely the process of thought. Yes. It was fitting. With a little thought, ad copy wouldn't even be hard to come up with, given a name like that. "Feel the Flame!" could be a subtitle of sorts. *I crack myself up. Crack! Ha!*

It didn't take long to portion the crystals into separate little baggies and stuff them in a pocket. Then the cleanup began. Washing everything and putting it back just as it had been before. Of course, no one would probably notice a few little anomalies—that had been proven in the past few weeks of tweaking the recipe. Last Tuesday the stirring rod had been left on the counter. Panic had almost set in the next day when the realization dawned, but no one else seemed to have noticed. Still, it was better to try to put everything back exactly as found to avoid raising suspicions. Stepping back, an assessment showed the room was once more set to rights.

With a lift of the beer can, and a salute to the empty chemistry room of North Sound Island's Cedar Harbor High

School, the earlier smirk turned into a laugh. "Here's to making my fortune off of all you little pukes!"

The doorknob was cool beneath a slightly sweaty palm. The door eased open with the barest of squeaks, but still the sound sent heartrate skyrocketing.

Calming breath. The hot ball of anxiety cooled.

As it should, the hallway remained empty.

The walk down the corridor, across the parking lot, and to the car parked in the shadows of the low madrona trees along the road leading up to the school seemed to take much longer than it should. But, as per usual, nothing. Everything lay silent and still right up to the moment of slipping back into the house and closing the door.

Head tilted to the wood, a sigh of relief slipped free.

One more batch had been made without detection. Figuring out a way to cook bigger batches would be necessary at some point. But for now...

Let the money start rolling in!

Chapter 2

Detective Case Lexington sank back against the driver's seat and propped his temple against one fist, eyeing his partner across the vehicle. "No way he's going to show. I think you spooked him."

A pink dawn breathed light against the bits of sky revealed between the 1950s-style homes on the downtown Everett street, a poignant reminder that he wouldn't be experiencing the comfort of his bed anytime soon.

Damian Packard stuffed another Dorito into his mouth and crunched with abandon. "He'll show."

Case checked the time and let his silence reiterate his belief that this was all a waste of good sleep.

Pack huffed. "I'm telling you the man can't stay away from this girl." He peered out the windshield at the blue house down the block where, all night long, he'd been promising that their perp would "arrive any minute." He noisily slurped the last drops of his Mountain Dew, finishing with a grin. "Yeah, he's taking his sweet time. But he'll be here."

Case smothered a yawn. "This going to be like the time that prostitute CI of yours promised to deliver us her cocaine-running pimp?" He couldn't keep the deprecating humor from his tone.

Pack winced at the reminder of that sting gone so terribly wrong, but only reiterated, "He'll show. And he'll have the goods. In fact," his eyes twinkled, "I'm willing to make a little wager. You?"

Case scrubbed at his face, wishing for nothing more than a hot shower and a shave to scrape away the irritating scruff coating his jaw. Boredom must be setting in after their ten-hour wait, because against his better judgment, he agreed with a shrug. "Sure. Terms?"

His partner chomped another chip and considered. "Dominguez doesn't show and I'll wash, vacuum, and detail our rig. He does show and you"—Pack scanned the shops along the street, then his gaze lit with mischief when it landed on the nail salon down a block and on one corner—"have to get a manicure."

Case laughed in spite of himself. "A manicure?"

"A manicure. In that little shop right there." Damian nodded in satisfaction, tossed out a leer of challenge, and munched down another chip. Several crumbs spilled onto his chest and he brushed them to the floor. "What do you say?"

Case scanned the dusty, sticky, stained, and fast-food-wrapper-littered interior of their stakeout van. The thing looked like a family with six teenagers had lived in it for a month. And if he did lose, all he'd have to do would be endure a manicure and the ribbing from the guys until the next prank gave them someone new to focus on. "Fine, you're on." He put out his fist for their signature bump-and-thump.

Pack arched a brow and made a fist but didn't touch him yet. "You have to get polish."

Case shook his head. "No way."

Pack nodded. "Clear will do. But the manicure has to include polish."

Case scanned the street. Dominguez still wasn't in sight. "Fine, but he has to show up in the next hour or the deal is off."

Pack bumped his fist. "Oh, this is going to be so good."

Saturday morning, Kyra Radell slung her bag over one shoulder and pressed the lock button on her Honda's remote. The car chirped a goodbye as she stepped onto the curb and stabbed her key into the door to *A Perfect Ten, Hands Down*. The scent of fresh brew from the coffee shop next door enticed her, but she'd just open up first and then call over her order.

Pushing into the shop, she turned on lights and the Open sign and stepped behind the counter to drop her purse into her cubby. She turned on the iPad beneath the register, which was set to stream Christian music from top artists through the digital speakers in each of the salon's corners. Pressing her hands into her lower back, she glanced around. Looked like Lainey had been busy this week. Her sister's salon was clean, but several bottles of polish were out of the color spectrum order that Lainey liked to keep them in, and one of the manicure tables still had yesterday's cloth on it.

She groaned a little, hoping that today wasn't going to be too busy or offer anything but the mundane. Packing for her upcoming move to North Sound Island was giving her enough stress and exhaustion this weekend. Yet, even through the fatigue, a little trill of excitement coursed through her.

She forced her mind back to the work. This was her last day and she wanted to do a good job for Lainey. She'd trained Marcy, her replacement, well, so going forward Lainey should be in good hands.

Kyra swept off the cloth and dropped it into the laundry basket they kept in the back. Taking up the disinfectant spray, she spritzed it over the surface and wiped down that table and each of the other three. If Lainey had forgotten to do one, she might have forgotten to do the others. Her sister had been a little frazzled since the birth of her twins. It must be hard wanting to rush home to them and her loving husband each night after a long day of work.

Kyra sighed. Not like she would know anything about that. But she was moving on and wasn't going to give that two-timing Mark Green another thought.

And come Wednesday, she would start her first day as a high school teacher. Just the thought revved up her excitement and tipped her lips into a smile. To land her dream job, and in the cozy community of Cedar Harbor in the San Juan Islands to boot, thrilled her to no end. Finally, all her years of education were going to pay off. She was going to speak love and encouragement and be a positive influence on all her students.

For Kingston. Because of Kingston. The thought of her brother and all that he'd put their family through threatened to put a damper on her mood. But she forcefully pushed the thoughts away. *Take every thought captive.* "Jesus, You are my reason for joy. Not any one person. Not any circumstance. It's because of You that I'm thrilled to minister to these new kids You are placing in my life." The prayer eased the threatening melancholy and she concentrated on being joyful.

Yes. She did a little happy dance right there in the store.

Life was looking up—even if Mark's picture was still tacked to the bull's-eye on her dart board.

The bell above the door jangled and she turned, rag and disinfectant still in hand, to greet the guest. She froze.

It wasn't like she'd never seen a man in the salon before, but this guy wasn't the business-suited type who normally came in with soft hands and pale, permanently-behind-a-desk skin.

His short-cropped messy spike was a light brown with natural blond highlights that proved he spent a good deal of time in the sun. As did the tan which emphasized dark-lashed eyes that were a pale color she couldn't quite make out from this distance. Thick brown stubble accentuated the angles of a very masculine jawline and the soft petulance of a mouth that looked anything but happy at the moment. He obviously didn't want to be here.

And she was gaping at him like he'd just stepped off the pages of *Beautiful People*.

The thought jarred her into action. "H-hi." She set the rag and disinfectant back into the cupboard and washed her hands at the sink, eyeing him over her shoulder. "What can I do for you this morning?"

The man raised his hand to scratch the back of his neck, studying her like he might bolt right back out the door. Dark brows slumped lower over those mesmerizing eyes.

She picked up the hand towel and spun to face him as she dried. Her attention dropped to the hand still propped against one of his hips. Broad blunt-tipped fingers with short clipped nails. Not unkempt, but also not hands that were normally manicured.

He's probably here to get something for his girlfriend. Of course such a specimen of male perfection would already be taken. Coffee would have to be her consolation after he left. *Coffee and a nice long daydream.*

She gave herself a mental shake. Hadn't she learned anything from Mark about a man's heart being more important than his looks? It was best she hurry him on his way. "Is there something in particular I can help you find?" She dropped the towel back onto the hook and stepped over to swap the misaligned bottles of polish.

The man glanced back out the glass door with an expression of longing and then took a breath and another full step into the salon. "I'm here to get a manicure." He almost winced after he said it.

Amusement tugged at her lips before she realized it and quickly pressed them together. "Okay, I just opened, but please"—she swept a gesture to her favorite station—"have a seat and I'll be right with you." His reasons for getting a mani were his own, she supposed, but she'd give up caffeine for a week to learn what had brought him here.

Case felt like a condemned prisoner as he straddled the seat she'd indicated. But now that his eyes were adjusted to the light of the interior, he let himself study the girl as she turned to gather some supplies. If he was a prisoner, she could be his jailer anytime. There could be worse ways to spend half an hour than looking at her. Much worse. She had a beauty that could make a man forget to breathe. Petite, with long legs zipped into calf-height brown boots. The pink scarf wrapped around her throat set off the frosty pink of full pouty lips to perfection.

Sinking into the chair across from him, she spread a towel on the table between them and laid a paper towel over that. She looked up and met his perusal.

He swallowed.

Light blue eyes brought to mind the topaz ring his sister wore all the time. Yes. Definitely. Light blue topaz outlined with blue-black sapphire.

"You can just rest both hands right here." She smoothed her hands over the table.

He followed her instructions, exercising all his self-control not to clench his fingers. If Dominguez wasn't such a lowdown drug runner, he could almost wish the guy hadn't shown up. But much to Pack's delight, Dominguez had shown up and tried to sneak into his girl's window only about fifteen minutes after their little bet.

The blonde bent her head over his hands and studied his

fingers. She had two thick braids wrapped around her head like an old-fashioned milkmaid.

She picked up a tool that looked a little like someone had glued sandpaper to a rounded paint stick. "So what do you want?"

Now that he'd seen her, he wanted something entirely different than he had when he walked in here, but of course he couldn't just blurt out that a date might be nice. He grinned despite himself. Pack was never going to let him hear the end of this. "I have no idea. I'm sort of here because I lost a bet."

One slim brow arched higher than the other. And a small smile lifted one corner of her mouth. "Ah. Well by all means let me end your torture and give you the quickest manicure ever."

"It has to include polish." He winced.

She gave a short laugh that fell more on the side of a giggle than outright humor.

How long had it been since he'd liked a sound that much? He couldn't remember.

"That must have been some bet."

"You have no idea." His ribs were still bruised from where Dominguez's bullet had connected with his flak jacket. Getting a manicure was only adding insult to injury.

Except for meeting her. To look into a face like that a man might be tempted to get a manicure every week. Heck. Every day.

She was still chuckling when she picked up the index finger on his right hand and started to file his nail.

Her head was so close, the fragrance of coconut and something else tantalized and made him want to lean nearer to determine the scent. He eased back in the chair before he did something stupid. Her fingers were slender with short nails painted a conservative pink that matched her scarf. Each thumbnail had a small diamond embedded in the polish at one side.

She finished filing the nails on his first hand and rested it in a little tub of warm, blue liquid while she went to work on the other.

Her skin against his was cool and he had the impulse to turn his hand over and capture her fingers between his own to warm them. He suppressed a roll of his eyes. It had been a long time since a woman had made him want to do that.

He needed a distraction. "What's your name?"

She looked up, brows peaked, as though surprised he'd spoken.

What could he say? Nerves brought out the interrogator in him. But more than that, he wanted to get to know her. Again, not something that was normal for him.

Apparently deciding it couldn't hurt to give him her name, she said, "My name's Kyra. And you are?"

"Case."

She gave a little nod of acknowledgement. "Nice to meet you, Case." Once more she resumed her concentration on his fingers. Now she placed his left hand into the tub and drizzled some sort of creamy looking goop onto each fingernail of his right and rubbed it into the base of his nails.

He searched for another benign question. "Do you like working here?"

She tilted her head and thought for a moment as she picked up a metal tool with a rounded paddle on one end. "Yeah, I guess I do. My sister owns this salon and I've just worked here to help her out on Saturdays."

So she had a sister. He wondered about any other... *important* people in her life. "You have any other family?"

She tucked the side of her lower lip between her teeth, a twinkle making the facets of her irises dance. "Just Roscoe."

His heart dropped but there was a hint of duplicity in the way she said the name that made him lean closer and ask, "And Roscoe is...?"

"Oh Roscoe is one of my best friends. He is always there for me. Always seems to know what I need before I need it."

"The perfect guy, huh?" *Has to be a dog. Please tell me it's a dog.*

Her sardonic smirk was in full bloom now. "He would be if he wasn't my sister's Pomeranian."

Bingo. He grinned. "The music is Christian." He lifted a finger toward one of the speakers. "You go to church around here?" He couldn't deny that his pulse quickened a little as he waited for her answer.

She tilted her head slightly and paused for a moment as though contemplating whether she could be revealing too much about herself to a stranger.

He realized he'd put his nose where it didn't belong. "I'm sorry. Don't mind me. I shouldn't—"

"No. It's fine. And the answer is yes. I do go to church down at Bethany Christian. But I got a second job, and will be moving. So I guess I'll have to find a church near my new home."

He wanted to pump his fist but resisted. It was the same large church that he went to on the Sundays he wasn't working a case. They had four services each week, so it wasn't any wonder that he didn't remember seeing her there. They probably attended at different times. But he didn't want to press for more information that would make her uncomfortable, so instead he took the conversation along its natural course. "And what's this other job?"

A passion leapt into her gaze that told him he'd found something she could expound on for hours. He knew that look. The one that said he was about to get a fount of information from his "grillee" as Pack would have called her. He was the griller. She was the grillee.

"I'm a teacher." She set to work scraping his cuticles back

from his nails with her little torture device and shrugged. "Well, I'm going to be. Just got hired this week and school starts on Wednesday."

"A teacher. Nice. What grade?"

"High school English."

"You are a high school English teacher?" He couldn't hide the incredulity in his tone. And he didn't even try to stop the next words that crossed his lips, because he suddenly wanted to see her blush, just once. He had a feeling it would be nice. "No English teacher of mine ever looked like you. Bet all the guys will be lining up to ask you for help with their papers."

Just as he'd hoped, a pretty pink touched her cheeks.

But she was all business and didn't retort to his flirting. "English and PE. It's a small school so I'll be doing both."

That statement set him back. If she was moving to a small school, it likely wasn't one around here. At least not a public school. But he couldn't very well ask her where she was moving to without coming across like a creepy stalker, now could he?

She worked her way around each cuticle with a little pair of clippers and then pumped some lotion into her hands and stood.

She started massaging his hand, working over each finger and then circling her thumbs into his palm and the muscled web of his hand. Her fingers interlaced with his and her slender fingers were strong as they slid up and down working the blood flow. But as good as the little massage felt, he realized he'd never been more aware of a woman than he was in that moment.

He let his gaze linger on her face as she reached to begin the massage on his left hand.

She worked over each finger and massaged strong circles into the heel and over his wrist, but didn't meet his gaze.

Small blue gemstones glittered in her ears. Ears that were

turning pink because he was staring like a love-struck teenager, he realized. He tore his gaze down to the cloth between them. "Sorry. You're very beautiful." He literally bit his tongue.

She cleared her throat and carefully set his hands next to each other. "Tell you what. I'm going to give your nails a quick buff that will give them shine, but won't require polish, how's that sound?"

"Uh, yeah, good by me."

She sat back down and set to work with another little tool that looked very similar to the first one, but was softer. He managed to contain the barrage of interrogation questions that pestered him for answers and she didn't offer any more information on her own.

Inside of ten minutes she had finished. "There, that should do you and satisfy your bet to your buddies." She offered a small smile that was a bit tight around the edges as she headed for the cash register.

He'd scared her with his forwardness. As he reached for his wallet and stopped by the front counter he said, "Listen, I'm really sorry. I didn't mean to be so forward, or to offend you."

She punched in some numbers before she tilted him a look. "First you compliment me. Then you apologize? Now I'm really offended." She let him know she was teasing with a rapid-fire wink.

His hopes rose. Maybe he hadn't blown this chance all to smithereens. And this might be his last chance to get that date. He held his debit card out to her. "So...since Roscoe seems to be the only other man in your life, would you care to join me for dinner sometime?"

She angled him a get-serious stare as she swiped his card through the reader.

He pasted on his most charming smile and gave her the look he'd used on countless undercover jobs to garner intel from sources of the female persuasion. "Come on. What can one date hurt? And you'll help me salvage my bruised ego with the guys."

She snorted inelegantly. "You bruised your little ol' ego all on your own. And for all I know, you could be a serial killer."

"A serial killer?" He thrust one hand over his heart. "You wound me, most grievous, my lady."

She laughed and handed him back his card and receipt. "No. Sorry. I am currently sworn off the two-timing, double-crossing, charm-wielding"—she pegged him with a pointed look—"species known as men."

He gave her a wince. "Last relationship was that bad, huh?" He tucked the items into his wallet and returned it to his pocket.

She folded her arms against the counter and leaned into them. "You have no idea."

"Well..." He matched her gesture, so he could meet her eye to eye. To his surprise she didn't pull back. He lowered his voice. "I will tell you that I'm neither of the first two items on your list. In fact, I'm a Bible-believing, church-attending, all around good guy. But..." He offered a shrug and a sly wink. "I might be accused of being charming every now and then."

"Well Mr. Bible-believing-church-attender, the answer is still no." Her dismissive smile widened. "Have a nice day, Case."

He eased back and tapped his finger onto the counter in the space between them. "You sure this is your last day? Or is that just something you tell the guys to keep them at bay?"

She laughed and raised two fingers. "Scout's honor it's my last day."

He tried to look dejected. "Well then, I guess I don't need to figure out a way to lose another bet this week. Don't suppose I could talk you into giving me your number?"

She hesitated, and for just the briefest of moments hope

soared, but then... "You're sweet and I'm flattered, but it's just not the right timing for me."

Deflated like a tire that had just run over a spike strip, he still had enough presence of mind to realize it was time to walk away while he could with his head held high. He offered a parting smile to indicate he harbored no grudge. "I understand. Really. And no hard feelings. All the best to you." And with that, he headed back to his car. As he slipped behind the wheel, he assessed his feelings and was surprised to find that, despite her rejection and his momentary deflation just a bit ago, he felt lighter and freer than he had in a very long time.

He shook his head at himself in the rearview mirror. *You're losing it, man.*

Chapter 3

Monday morning, Case sat at his desk and glanced over the meeting agenda for the day. He'd actually managed to make it to church yesterday, but though he'd looked for Kyra, he hadn't found her in the service he'd attended.

Across the room, his partner cleared his throat. Pack was studying him with a speculative gleam in his eyes.

Case searched his memory of the past few moments. There was no way he was going to let on to his partner that the manicure hadn't been as torturous as the fiend had hoped it would be. He didn't think he'd done anything to give it away. But Pack was like a hound on a scent when it came to sniffing out new information.

Case snapped the file he'd been perusing closed. "What?" He went for the nonchalant approach.

Pack steepled his fingers against his lips. "You seem mighty chipper for a man who looked like he was condemned to the gallows Friday after work. Let's see your *hand*iwork." He leered, and chuckles emanated from several desks in their vicinity.

Stalking over to his partner's desk, Case slapped his palms down, fingers splayed.

Pack's eyes narrowed. "That's not polish!"

Case tipped his head toward his nails. "Look again. Are they shiny?"

A noncommittal nod was his only answer.

Straightening, Case stuffed his fingers into his armpits and leaned into his heels. "Yes, they are shiny. Therefore they are *polished.* End of story." He turned and headed for the meeting room glowering at anyone who even dared to smirk in his direction.

It gave him great satisfaction when a moment later Captain Mick Danielson walked into the room, scanned the occupants, and then thrust his head back out the door and yelled, "Packard, put your donut down and get your butt in here! You're late!"

Pack moseyed in a few moments later licking icing from his fingers. Everyone knew that Captain Danielson was more bark than bite.

Danielson pinned Pack with a look that would have made a newer cop tremble in his boots. "Can we commence now? That alright by you?"

Easing into casual repose against a desk, Pack nodded. "Sorry, Cap. I'll try to do better next time."

Danielson shook his head and scanned the tablet in his hands. "Okay, so here's the lowdown. High school out on North Sound Island has been having a big drug problem. At the end of last year, a kid at a local party ODed. Died just before graduation. That was the first incident. But there were two more cases last month. Both kids made it, but it was close. This is your basic meth with a high booster of some sort that their local coroner hasn't been able to nail down just yet." The captain looked up and scanned the room. "On Saturday another body was found down near the ferry docks." The captain examined his notes. "Mason Green. Kid would have been a senior this coming year. The thing is"—he dropped the tablet on the table in front of him—"none of the kids are wanting to talk. So whoever they are getting this stuff from has a pretty tight rein on their loyalty. The local sheriff, Holden Parker, reached out for assistance and wants a team that won't be recognizable to the locals. Our unit has been tasked with setting up an undercover operation to see what we can find out. Lexington, you're up to bat, and you are going to need parents. Well...a parent." He spread his arms in a *ta-da* motion, leaning back as though accepting applause from a crowd.

Case sat up in his chair. He was ready to do his job—anytime he could put a slimy drug dealer in jail was a good time, but... "I'm going in as a student?"

Danielson nodded and dropped a file in front of him. "Here's your cover. I get the pleasure of being your father, so, I hope you'll be a well-behaved young man, and"—he grinned and bent down to pat Case's cheek patronizingly—"that you won't cost me an arm and a leg for manicures."

Everyone in the room busted up laughing, including Case. That was one thing he'd learned early on in the force...if you couldn't take a ribbing and still smile, you'd better find a different job.

Still chuckling, Case rolled his eyes and ducked away from Danielson's teasing. "I'll do my best, *Pops*."

Danielson turned to Packard. "Damian, since I'll be out in the field, you'll be running point back here in the office and doing most of the communicating with the sheriff on the island."

Pack nodded.

"Alright, school starts on Wednesday so let's move, people. We have a lot of work to do before then. We are going to start our investigation in the high school itself. Likely the seller is one of the students. Or at least someone close to one. But if we have to we'll expand our search from there. Any questions?" No one seemed to have any so the captain dismissed the meeting with his typical brusque instructions to each person on what he wanted them focused on.

Case sighed and flipped open his file. Might as well get to know the new him.

Probably was a good thing that he hadn't been able to change the mind of the pretty Miss Kyra about that date.

Wednesday morning, Kyra stood in the teacher's lounge and pulled in a long slow inhale before forcing it out between pursed lips. Her first class started in fifteen minutes. To say she was nervous would be like saying this island was surrounded by water.

This was her life's dream. She so wanted to make a good impression, not only on her co-workers, but also on the teens she felt certain she'd been sent here to reach. Love was so lacking in most kids' lives these days. And she knew beyond a shadow of a doubt that God had called her to teach so she could help kids see how special and wonderful and important each of them were, even in the grand scheme of things.

She was thankful to have found a house to rent on the island just this past Monday. She had already been partially packed for a move in case she did find something before school started. But still, after the last few days of whirlwind packing, cleaning her old place in Everett, and moving out here via several trips on the ferry, she was exhausted. In the end though, it felt good to finally be seeing her dreams come to fruition.

She smoothed her hands over her turquoise blouse and scanned it once more for wrinkles. Her black slacks had been hanging in her closet so they hadn't given her too hard of a time at the ironing board this morning. But her top had been suffocating in the bottom of a box for days and she just hoped in her haste to iron it she hadn't missed something obvious, even though she'd double checked several times already. The suede turquoise Jeffery Campbell booties were probably a bit much, and she'd be lucky not to have cramps in her toes by the end of the day since it had been an age since she'd worn such high heels. But they'd been the first shoes she could find that matched her outfit and besides she wanted to make a good impression on the kids.

"Hey, you must be the new teacher?" The masculine voice had a slight southern drawl and was warm enough to send a shiver up her spine.

She spun around. The man wore dark gray slacks and a green striped button-down with a solid green tie knotted smartly at his throat. A gold tie tack glimmered against the green silk.

He smiled and stretched out his hand. "I'm Simon Hall. Shorty to my friends. I'm the chemistry teacher here."

Kyra took his hand, noting that in her heels she did have to look down at him just a bit and she was only five four. He had nice brown eyes behind his glasses. Just not as nice as the dark-lashed gray-green eyes of the man she hadn't quite been able to get out of her mind since Saturday. She forcefully thrust Case's image aside and squeezed Simon's hand. "Kyra Radell. Yes, I'm the new English and PE teacher."

His gaze skimmed to her heels and he grinned as he pushed his glasses up on his nose with one finger. "Hope you won't try to teach gym class in those things."

She chuckled. "No, I have gym clothes." She glanced at the clock on the wall. "It's really nice to meet you, but I'd better hurry to my classroom."

"Yeah, me too, I guess. But listen. Just be aware that a lot of the kids are a bit high-strung these days what with all that's going on. So if anyone gets rowdy, or whatever, my classroom is just across the hall from yours. I'm happy to help, anytime."

Kyra searched her memory for anything the hiring committee might have said that could correlate to his statement but came up blank. "Going on?"

The man's eyes widened a bit. "You haven't heard? Oh man. I'm sorry to have to be the one to tell you. One of our students was killed just a few days ago. He ODed on an as-of-yet unidentified drug." He pulled a face. "Kids. You tell them and tell them how dangerous those kinds of things are. And..." He paused to sniff and blink a couple times. "I'm sorry. He was a good kid. Too much potential to go out like that. Anyhow...as you can see, the whole community is a bit shaken up."

Kyra's heart pinched. "I'm very sorry to hear it. Thank you for letting me know. I'll call on you if I need anything."

As if her first-day jitters weren't bad enough! This was the very reason she'd wanted to be a teacher. To prevent these very kinds of things if she could. God had dropped her right into the heart of the battlefield. She hoped she'd be up to the challenge.

"Right. All the best for your first day."

She nodded her thanks and left him to collect his emotions. But some of the excitement had just been sapped from her. That poor man. And these poor kids. He seemed nice enough, she thought, as she wove her way through the crowded hallway, twisting this way and that between kids who were in various states of animation. Some seemed oblivious to what had happened over the summer and chattered animatedly, thrilled that school was starting up. Others could barely seem to find the energy to sling their backpacks into their lockers, and she saw a couple of kids consoling each other, tears glistening on their cheeks.

The knife of a memory threatened to bring on a headache, but she pushed the thoughts away. Not today. She didn't have the emotional energy to deal with thoughts of Kingston's death right now.

Lord, I need Your strength. Help me to push past the pain and find the hurting and the broken. Help me to be Love in their lives. Let them see You in me. Let them find hope in You. She didn't have time for more of a prayer because she was at her classroom and several students were already lounging in the desks she'd arranged to her liking the evening before. The drain of what she'd just learned from Simon Hall, combined with the reminder of just how late she'd been here, made her want to yawn. She resisted, and offered the students a friendly smile instead. At her desk, she opened up her PowerPoint and tossed up another quick prayer that all her technology would work this morning.

The first bell rang and more students sauntered through the door. Two boys came in, took one look at her, and then set to slapping each other on the back and fist bumping as they spoke low behind their hands and scanned her up and down.

To hide her embarrassment, she turned and picked up the remote for her classroom's projector and focused on powering it on. She got so tired of people taking one look at her and categorizing her as nothing more than a nice object to ogle. Still, maybe it was her fault for dressing up so much on the first day. And she probably should have pinned her long wavy hair into a bun. She'd take care of that during the break between the classes.

Second bell rang and the classroom settled into an expectant quiet. She'd bet that wouldn't last much past the first couple of days.

She folded her hands. "Good morning class and welcome to Senior English. My name is Miss Radell, and I look forward—"

A male student bustled through the door, baseball cap on backwards and books askew in his arms. He was looking down at a paper on his top book as he came through the door, but glanced up as he entered. "I'm sorry. I'm new and—"

Kyra's jaw dropped. She couldn't help herself. Because the wide-eyed boy staring back at her was Case, the man who'd been at the salon on Saturday. One ankle wobbled as she stepped behind her desk and pretended to straighten some papers. She racked her brain.

He was a student? She would have sworn he was at least her age or older last Saturday.

She pushed back a wash of lightheadedness. This could get her fired before she even got started!

Had she flirted too openly? Only a little.

Had she said anything untoward? Not that she could recall.

Thank God she'd refused his request for a date! What a mess that would have been!

The silence was stretching, and she realized several in the classroom were eyeing her strangely. She leveled him with a look, and if her emotions were any measurement it was none too friendly. But just before she spoke she reminded herself he'd said he was new here. "Your name is?"

"Uh, Case, ma'am." If the paleness around his wide eyes was any indication, he was just as shocked to see her as she was to see him.

But she wasn't the one who had portrayed herself as an adult and hit on an older woman. She felt her eyebrows lift. "Case, do you have a last name?"

"Sheridan."

Something stirred a bit of unease. Had that been the same name on his credit card? She'd been so flustered by his compliments and teasing there at the end that she didn't remember even glancing at his last name on the card.

"Well, Mr. Sheridan, since you are new, and I understand how navigating around an unfamiliar facility might make you late, just this once I'll let it pass. In the future, please do your best to be on time?"

He swallowed and nodded.

She held her hand out to the last remaining empty desk— in the front row—then snatched it back when she noticed how it trembled. "Please, take your seat."

CHAPTER 4

Case was one of the first students out of the classroom as soon as they were dismissed. Grinding his teeth, he stuffed his head inside his locker and scrunched his eyes shut.

He forced himself to go over every detail of their first meeting. Had he said anything to her about being a cop? No, he didn't think so. They'd mostly talked about her work.

Still, Captain Danielson was going to kill him. The excuse of being a nineteen-year-old senior was always his cover for his fairly heavy stubble. But how did one cover for "pretending" to be an adult? He needed to think of a way to salvage this situation and he needed to do it quickly before she started asking questions about him. They could potentially read her in, but that was dangerous, both for her and for their op. And what did they know about her anyhow? They'd have to do a full background workup on her. Had she been in the area long enough to be the one supplying drugs to the kids? Everett wasn't so far away that it was totally out of the question, even if it was implausible.

He slapped his locker shut and slammed his palm against it. What were the odds that of all the places in the world she got a job here and that he'd happened to walk into her sister's salon last Saturday?

He pinched the bridge of his nose as he fell in with the stream of kids moving down the hallway.

As if seeing her in English class wasn't enough, she was also his advanced PE teacher. She'd changed her hair by then—had it pulled back into a severe ponytail that she probably hoped disguised her looks but didn't. As she introduced the class and talked about tennis, the first sport they'd be covering, the two guys in front of him kept whispering to each other and making lewd gestures. He wanted to thump their heads together.

Instead, he saw it for the opportunity it was and muttered just loud enough for them to hear but maybe think he was talking to himself, "I could score me some o' that." He ground his teeth and reminded himself this was all just part of his job.

The boys thumped each other's shoulders, laughing like he'd just told the best joke of the year. One of them spoke over his shoulder. "Get in line, bro."

They all laughed.

And Case was satisfied. He'd back off now for a bit. Let them wonder about him for a few days before he laid his cover story on them. Show a little attitude in classes, maybe sleep a little too.

Some agents went under and pressured any kid they could to get them drugs so they could make some arrests and make the op look good. But one thing he appreciated about his boss was his emphasis that they never pressure any of the kids to get them drugs. Case agreed with that philosophy one hundred percent. If a kid was already dealing, that was one thing, but he never wanted one of his investigations to corrupt a kid who was just trying to impress and befriend him.

Miss Radell paired them off into teams for doubles and disbursed them to the outdoor courts behind the gym.

Case ended up paired with a bouncy, talkative, gum-chewing blonde that he might have thought was cute back in high school. She batted her eyelashes invitingly, giving him a once-over. But he only nodded a greeting.

There were several strict rules undercover. And relationships fell under those rules. Undercover or not, it was still a crime to seduce an underage kid, so relationships were off the books. Team sports were also prohibited to officers, so while athleticism came naturally to him, he generally toned down his natural abilities a lot to keep from being prodded to join a team. Especially in small schools like this where every body on the court often counted.

The team across from him served, and his partner Chloe returned the ball. He could tell by the way she moved that she was athletic and likely part of the popular crowd. Assessing, always assessing. Was it the popular kids in this school doing the drugs? Sometimes it was and sometimes, surprisingly, that crowd spurned the drugs and it was the outcasts who turned to them. Most of the time it was a mixture from each segment of the school. But Chloe was likely to be a friend to make. The trick would be doing that and keeping it purely platonic.

The ball was headed his way and he tripped over his feet, careening to the cement and missing the ball altogher.

"Wow." Chloe chomped her gum and grinned at him. "For being such a McDreamy you sure can't play tennis."

He pushed himself up to a sitting position. "Sorry you got stuck with me."

She giggled. "Don't sweat it. I'm Chloe Schumacher, by the way."

"Yeah, I caught your name." He winked at her. Hopefully it came across as friendly and not too flirtatious. "I'm Case—"

"Case, are you okay?" Miss Radell was suddenly by his side and stretching down a hand to help him up.

"Sheridan," he finished saying to Chloe. And since a teenage guy would likely not appreciate looking like he needed help from a female teacher, he spurned her hand and hopped to his feet. "It's all good, Miss Radell. Thanks for asking."

She was studying him quizzically with those delicate brows

of hers all scrunched together, which returned his dilemma over what to do about her to the front of his mind. She hadn't said anything to him—at least not yet—and it wasn't likely she would bring up their past meeting to any of her colleagues because then there would have to be an investigation and he doubted she'd want that.

So he probably had a little bit of time. For now, he would just let things slide and see what happened. At least until he had time to talk to Mick. And, oh boy, Mick was going to let him have it but good about this blunder.

The other kids on their court were all looking at them now.

Kyra gave her head a little shake, then reached out a hand. "Let me see your racket for a minute."

He handed it over and she proceeded to show him how to hold it, and swing it, and slide his feet across the court so he wouldn't trip again.

Case resisted a grunt of frustration. Sometimes this job really wasn't fair. Having to look like a klutz in front of this beautiful woman was going to try him sorely.

With a smile, she handed him back his racket and turned her attention to another student, and Case resumed his position on the court. He made the next two swings count. He couldn't help himself.

But Kyra Radell wasn't paying a bit of attention.

When Case got home from the school, Captain Danielson was waiting for him—*Mick,* Case reminded himself. The man had insisted on the informality while they were under together. The living room of the house the department had rented for them was small, and currently cluttered with papers and file folders. Mick's laptop was on the coffee table before him, and a plate of cake and cup of coffee sat to one side.

The captain grinned. "Welcome home, son. How was your day? Need me to make you a snack?"

Case chuckled but didn't respond in kind. After moving a map of the island so he could dump his backpack onto the recliner, he turned to face his boss. "We may have a problem."

Captain Danielson immediately dropped his act. "Already? What is it?"

"Believe it or not, one of my teachers is a woman who was working at the nail salon I went to on Saturday."

Mick cursed. "Seriously? That can't be a coincidence can it? You think she knows something?"

Case shook his head. "I didn't even know about this op till Monday morning. And she did tell me on Saturday that she'd just gotten a new job as a teacher, she just didn't say where."

Mick pegged him with a look. "Don't tell me you hit on her!"

Case rubbed the back of his neck. "Okay. I won't."

The captain cursed again and kicked out at a chair.

Case tried for a soothing tone. "I'm pretty sure it's only a crazy coincidence, but we'd better do a full workup on her, anyhow."

"Most of that's already done. What's her name?" Mick strode to the map Case had tossed over some stacks of papers and moved it to one side.

"Radell. Kyra Radell."

The captain fingered through some folders and produced a thin one. "Here it is. This is all we could find on her."

Case flipped open the folder, for some reason feeling a little like he was snooping in an area he didn't belong. But this was for an op. Born in Kirkland, an Eastside suburb of Seattle, she'd been raised right here in Washington. Her parents still lived in Kirkland. Only one sister—she'd mentioned her when he'd been at the salon the other day. But she'd had a brother who'd died back in 2010.

He lowered the folder and pondered... Kyra was about his age, a little younger. That would put her around her freshman year in high school when her brother died. "Did we learn how her brother died?"

"Death report is in there somewhere. I think it was suicide."

Case's heart sank as he flipped through the pages. Sure enough. Her brother had been two years older than her and had killed himself by hanging. Processing that gave him the urge to track her down and tell her how sorry he was for her loss.

He shook the thought away and turned back to his perusal of her file. A long list of acting credits from several theaters during her high school years... He pondered... When she was younger, had her dream been to become an actress? What had made her want to teach? The acting had stopped abruptly mid-2010. That might answer those questions.

She'd graduated from Northwest University in Kirkland two years previous with a double major in theater arts and education. Since then she'd been working as a substitute teacher throughout Snohomish County and working at her sister's salon on the weekends, just as she'd told him. She had only two traffic tickets ever. And no criminal history of any kind.

Case closed the folder and tossed it on top of the stack. "None of this raises any red flags. It all matches everything she's told me. Today was her first day at the school, so the likelihood that she's our perp is slim to none. But she recognized me in class today. And I'm afraid she might start asking questions. So...what do we do about that?" He braced for whatever blast of ire Mick was about to lay on him.

But Mick only blew out a breath and scrubbed his hands over his face. "For now, we sit on it. Keep an eye on her. If you have to read her in, you do it, but I'd like to put it off for as long as possible if we can."

Case nodded, thankful for the confirmation of his own earlier conclusions. "Yes, sir."

"Meantime..." Mick gestured to the remaining folders in the stack. "Grab a folder and get to work."

Inwardly, Case groaned. "First, where's the rest of that cake?"

They were in for a long night.

Alone at her desk in her classroom, Kyra fiddled with a pencil and frowned at the data on her computer screen.

They were a few days into the school year now and she still hadn't decided what she ought to do about Case Sheridan.

The truth was, she'd really rather just put her head in the sand and pretend that the kid had never come to Lainey's salon and hit on her, but the more she'd watched him over the past few days, the more red flags had been raised.

The kid was putting on an act of some kind.

Case had been late to PE today, and he'd fallen asleep in English class yesterday. And she'd heard that he'd gotten detention from Principal Vaughan yesterday for disrespect and backtalk. Yet, when she'd called on him today to participate in the discussion about Beowulf, his answers had been insightful and precise.

She'd really only stayed late at the school to grade some pop quizzes she'd handed out today, but hadn't been able to get her mind off the disparity in the kid's personality. So she'd decided to pull up his school records. And those were doing nothing to ease her concerns. The boy had been to more schools than most military brats. And at each and every one he'd had discipline problems. So how was it that he'd come across as such a responsible adult when she'd interacted with him at the salon the other day?

She took her eyes from the computer screen to rub at the

headache that she now realized had been pulsing behind her browbone for quite some time. She blinked at the darkness of her classroom. No wonder she had a headache. She'd been staring at the glow of her screen in a completely dark room for who knew how long.

She grabbed the bottle of water from her desk and the bottle of Tylenol from her drawer. After tossing down two pills, she angled her computer screen toward the light switch she knew was over by the door to illuminate her way through the desks.

As she slowly maneuvered through the room, she let her thoughts return to the problem of Case Sheridan. In all likelihood, she was just upset with herself for being taken in by a kid the way she had, but she never wanted another family to suffer like her family had suffered after the way they'd lost Kingston. She owed it both to herself and to Case to look into his odd behavior more fully.

She was just reaching for the switch when a loud crash sounded from somewhere in the school. She froze and peered through the wired glass inset in her door. The only room she could see was Simon's across the hall.

His door was solid steel like her own, with only a small rectangle of wired glass at the top.

Was that a flash of light in his room?

She smiled. He'd probably done the same thing as her. Stayed late, realized it just now and headed for his light switch, only to knock something over.

Score one for not being klutzy.

She laughed and flipped on her classroom lights—maybe some of the illumination would seep into his room and allow him to find his own door and switch. Opening her door, she called out, "Simon, is that you? I only just realized myself how late it is."

Silence was the only response.

She frowned. Maybe he'd hurt himself? Had the crash she'd heard been him falling?

She started across the hall. "Are you okay? Do you need some help cleaning up?"

More silence.

Worry seeped in. What if he had knocked himself out or something? She might need to call for medics, but she'd left her phone back on her desk. She should grab it right quick, just in case. She rushed back into her classroom, snatched the phone off her desk, and then jogged back across the hall.

"Simon?" she tried once more.

Still no reply.

Her heart thumped against her sternum. What was going on?

She pushed down on his door handle, but the room was locked. Odd. Had the crash really come from this room? She only now realized that she'd assumed it was from this room because she'd seen the light. Had she really seen a light?

She stood on her tiptoes and peered into the classroom, but everything was pitch black.

It only took a moment to turn on the flashlight on her phone. She shone it through the little window, searching the room for anyone who might be hurt inside. But nothing seemed out of the ordinary.

Simon's desk sat at the back corner of the room—a mirror of the way she'd set up her own classroom. And she could see most of the floor between his desk and the door. She didn't see anyone, collapsed or otherwise. So unless someone had fallen behind one of the lab tables, or was pressed right against this door, there was no one in that room.

A prickle of unease tightened the skin along the back of her neck. Where had the sound come from then? And why had she thought she'd seen light in here?

Across the room, one of the heavy curtains at one of the windows fluttered inward, and that was when she saw the broken glass on the floor just below it.

A breath of relief whooshed from her. Simon had left one of the windows in his classroom open and likely a breeze had blown in and knocked the curtain into a beaker which had crashed onto the floor. Since his room was on the third floor of the high school, he probably often left a window open to air out the chemical smells. Maybe the flash of light had been nothing more than a car passing on the road outside the school.

Relieved to have her stressful little adventure fizzle into nothing more than a breeze, she turned back to her classroom with a roll of her eyes. Only she would get all hyped up over absolutely nothing.

Back at her desk, she stared once more at the records of one Case Sheridan. Hyped up over nothing. Maybe she was doing the same with Case. What kid wouldn't have social issues if he was dragged from school to school sometimes multiple times a year? His prank on her at the salon last Saturday had probably been nothing more than a bored kid seeing if he could really pass himself off as an adult. Likely practicing to see if he could get himself into a club with a fake ID, or something like that.

She blew out a breath. Maybe she was making a mountain out of a molehill, but still, she would keep an eye on him. However, for now, she'd let things ride.

Lord, please just don't let him hurt himself, because if I'm wrong I don't think I'd ever be able to forgive myself.

With that decision made, she pulled her purse from where she'd left it in her bottom drawer, locked up her classroom, set the alarm on the school just as she'd been taught, and headed for her car in the parking lot.

Another layer of relief washed over her when she noted that Simon's lime-green Corvette was not in the parking lot. In fact, her car was the only one left. She released her last shred of concern over his fate.

It really had just been the wind in his classroom.

Chapter 5

The metal of the chemistry room door pressed cold against a back damp with sweat and made the shirt stick uncomfortably. Knees curled to chest, quaked. Arms wrapped tight around them shook. The rapid rocking—forward, back, forward, back—did nothing to bring ease.

An all-too-familiar terror squirmed and writhed like a can full of fishing worms. Almost caught! Was it safe to move yet? What had that new teacher been doing here so late, anyhow?

Anger surged. Clenched fists banged the floor and pain radiated a reminder that flesh couldn't conquer concrete. All the effort and time and work to get to this point could have been lost in one moment! No one was supposed to be in the school at this hour! No one!

Careless! Why were you so careless? Always living up to what Father predicted.

Rocking. Rocking. Rocking.

"No!" The word emerged savage and hoarse.

Father was not right. And only a few more batches of Fire were going to prove that. It wasn't easy to make it in this world, but there was almost enough money now. Almost enough to start buying the equipment needed so larger batches could be made at home. Things would be much safer that way. After all, no one ever came to visit. And afterward, all the money would be free and clear.

Save it! Spend it! Vacation on it. The choices would be endless. A smile pleaded for release.

Just a few more months to freedom and affluence.

The rocking stopped. The arms eased. The promise of tomorrow lit hope deep inside.

But until then, what to do about the new teacher? Couldn't have her falling into a pattern of staying late at the school. That just wouldn't do. Had her car been in the parking lot a bit ago?

The floor pressed icily against scrambling knees, and a quick peek out the window revealed her, illuminated in the glow of the parking lot lights, just getting into her car.

A guttural grunt of disgust escaped.

Stupid. Stupid!

The car had been there the whole time. It was too easy to grow lazy and relaxed, obviously. Much too easy.

What if there'd been no time to lock the door?

Stupid! Stupid!

A sweep of lights crossed the curtains at the windows and the low hum of Kyra Radell's engine and crunch of her tires dissipated into the distance.

A breath eased through pursed lips. *She's gone.* No more danger.

For now, cooling and collecting this batch took priority. And next time a more careful scan of the area would be in order before coming in to cook. That and being more careful with the glass lab equipment.

Beaker. Glass stirring rod. Thermometer. Everything lay shattered on the floor.

Careless!

The broken glass begged to be cleaned up, but Radell would say something in the morning so it was best to leave it in shattered shards. The problem was...it would have traces of

Fire on it. Would they notice and be curious enough to test it? That couldn't be risked!

What to do?

Another beaker from the next station over caught a glint of moonlight as the curtain from the window—opened earlier to let out the fumes—wafted inward on a breeze. And just like that the solution presented itself.

A sigh of relief freed the last of the tension..

All was not lost. Not even remotely.

Father was wrong again.

Thursday morning, Kyra sat at her desk during her first-hour English period and studied her classroom. Students were supposed to be working on a report but Chloe Schumacher had been on her phone for the past fifteen minutes.

Kyra had determined not to overreact. The kids were supposed to be working on reports and she'd waited to see if the girl had simply wanted to check something on the internet right quick. But Kyra's dread mounted as it became clear that she was going to have to say something. Confrontation had never been her strong suit. Her heart was to reach her students with kindness and lure them into a love of learning, not badger and bash and demand from them in a way that would quash all the joy that being a life-long student could provide.

How did she go about challenging the girl to do better at her school work without putting a barrier between them? And without building a fire beneath the already steaming cauldron of insolence Chloe seemed to carry with her everywhere she went? The last thing Kyra wanted to do was set a pattern that would result in a year-long battle with the girl.

Most of the other students appeared to be working diligently, even Case Sheridan, miracle of miracles. So now was probably an okay time to leave the classroom for a few seconds.

Kyra stood. "Chloe?"

The girl looked up, rapidly shoving her phone into her backpack.

Kyra offered a smile. "May I speak to you in the hallway for a moment?"

Chloe rolled her eyes but stood with a gesture that made it clear she didn't think she had much choice and exited the classroom.

Taking a deep breath, Kyra followed her out.

Chloe leaned against the wall, arms folded and one foot propped up behind her.

Kyra let the disrespectful pose pass. Instead she tried to find some common ground. She pulled her own new red iPhone from the back pocket of her jeans and held it up for the girl to see.

Chloe looked a bit confused. Her gaze darted back in the direction of her desk where she'd just shoved her own phone into her backpack.

Kyra smiled. Good, catching her off guard might be the key to gaining the girl's respect. "This one is mine. Not yours. You got the new iPhone too? How do you like it?"

Understanding sapped some of the hardness from the girl's stance. "Yeah. It's pretty cool."

"I really like the new camera. It has some great new updates, doesn't it?" Kyra felt like she couldn't stretch out this olive branch much farther.

Chloe shrugged noncommittally. "Yeah. I said it was cool."

One more try. "What do you like best about it?"

Chloe only shrugged again. "I don't know."

Okay... So much for attempting to establish some rapport. Maybe it was just time to bring this to a close. She didn't want to be out of her classroom for much longer anyhow. "So here's the thing..." Kyra tucked her own phone back into her pocket. "I'm really not that hard of a teacher. But when I give an assignment *and* give you time in class to work on it, I expect you to be working and not just surfing on your phone. Were you doing research for your paper?"

Chloe hesitated and Kyra could see dilemma shining in the girl's eyes. Would she tell the truth?

After only a moment, the girl shook her head.

Kyra was relieved to see that she had chosen the better part of valor. She offered the girl another smile. "Well thank you for being honest. I really appreciate that. I'm going to let it go this time, but I want your word that from now on you'll make better use of your time in the classroom."

Chloe nodded. "Yes, ma'am."

Kyra stretched a hand toward the classroom door. "Thank you. You may return to your seat."

Chloe's expression registered surprise that she had let her off so easily. But after only a split second of hesitation, she bolted back into the classroom.

Once the girl was out of sight, Kyra let the wall take her weight, relieved to have the confrontation over with. Hopefully, Chloe would rise to the challenge and Kyra wouldn't later regret her leniency.

Thanking the Lord for an easy first battle-of-the-wills, Kyra turned to open her classroom door.

"You handled that really well."

Kyra paused and turned to face Simon who stood across the hall with his hands thrust into the pockets of his slacks. Today he wore a turquoise shirt and matching tie. The man always dressed classy.

She widened her eyes and blew at her hair, presenting a picture of precarious sanity.

He laughed. "Don't let them send you to the looney bin. Try to remember back to when you were a teen"—he swept a glance from her head to her toes and back again—"not that long ago."

She should laugh. Maybe even blush at his compliment. But the truth was, thinking back to her teen years was something she rarely tortured herself with. Those had been sad, confusing years that she tried to think about as little as possible now that she was past them. Having a brother who committed suicide had sent an explosion right into the heart of their family as surely as though someone had dropped a bomb in their living room.

She chose instead to change the subject. "Did you have a broken beaker in your room this morning?"

Simon looked surprised. "I did. How did you know?"

She laughed. "I was in my classroom last night about ten o'clock when I heard it break. I meandered over but didn't see anything out of the ordinary except that a window was open. It must have gotten knocked off the ledge by the curtain."

"Could be, I suppose. Well... I just escorted a student down to chat with our illustrious leader." He stretched his chin in the direction of the principal's office on the bottom floor. "I'd better get back inside." Another tip of his head indicated his classroom.

Kyra nodded and pointed to her own door. "Me too."

Just then a student poked his head out of Simon's classroom. "Mr. Hall, my beaker seems to be missing."

Simon turned to face the student. "Must be the one that got broken last night."

The kid shook his head. "I don't know. Kyle and Marissa are missing a bunch of things from their station too—a beaker, a glass stirring rod, and their thermometer. But I'm only missing a beaker."

Simon touched the boy's shoulder, directing him back into the classroom as he gave Kyra a farewell gesture. "Well, let's see if we can figure out who needs what."

Something about the exchange tugged for Kyra's attention as she stepped back into her own classroom, but two boys were having a spitball fight that demanded her immediate intervention. And by the time the bell had rung for the period to be over and she considered the incident again, she couldn't remember what had bothered her about it.

She gave a self-deprecating chuckle and massaged her temples, willing away the headache that threatened to take over.

Only twenty-three and she was already losing her mind.

It was the end of the day and her stomach rumbled for dinner, but Kyra put it off for a few more minutes. After the day she'd just had, it was clear that she needed to do something drastic to get the kids interested in the medieval literature she so wanted them to enjoy.

Perhaps a little recitation? Or...playacting on the kids' parts? Yes! Maybe tomorrow she would give them all a break, have them spend a few minutes writing up their own medieval scripts, and then they could perform them for each other. What kid wouldn't enjoy writing their own story about dragon slayers, knights, and maidens fair?

She had a trunk of theatrical supplies with a lot of fun props left over from her own days in theatre. She dragged it to the front of the classroom and opened the lid. Pulled out a stick horse and a golden crown.

With a giggle and a glance around, she settled the crown on her head and "mounted" the horse. "Trotting" a few paces across the front of the classroom, she thrust one fist into the air and proclaimed, "*Beowulf* will never seem more interesting to any students anywhere!"

"Glad to see that my newest hire is taking her job so seriously." A low chuckle emanated from behind her.

With a gasp, Kyra spun around, tugging the crown from her head and dropping the stick horse in her haste. "Principal Vaughan!" Her face blazed. "I was just brainstorming ways to make medieval literature more interesting to twenty-first-century kids." Gathering up the horse, she hurried over to the trunk and plopped the props inside. "What can I do for you?"

The man's smile was genuine and held no mockery. "Please. I'm always happy to see a teacher go above and beyond."

Kyra laughed nervously, still embarrassed at having been caught playacting. "Guilty as charged, I guess."

The man stepped further into the classroom and set his large satchel briefcase onto the closest student desk. "It's actually the reason I came up here. I was just heading home, but saw your car was still in the parking lot, and that reminded me I noticed your code closed out the school alarm quite late the other night."

"I was here late grading some papers. Is...there a problem with that?" Kyra wasn't sure what to make of the man's comments.

"No! No. Not at all. It's just that I wanted to caution you to be careful, at least until the police can figure out this whole drug fiasco. With all that's been going on lately I'd hate for something to happen to one of my teachers." He smiled. "That's all. Just be careful okay? Maybe grade papers at home for a time instead of here? And leave when the parking lot is busy, or at the very least while it's still light outside." He gave a pointed look to her classroom windows where she suddenly noticed how dark it had become.

Relieved that she wasn't in trouble for trying to do a good

job, Kyra started to gather her things. "Of course. Thank you for thinking of my safety. I was just getting ready to leave."

"Well, good. Mind if I walk you out?"

"Of course not. Thank you."

The man chatted amiably with her as they made their way from the building, set the school alarm, and walked through the darkness to the parking lot. He waited patiently while she dug for her keys, and smiled kindly when she thanked him again for his concern.

"See you tomorrow," was all he said as he headed for his own car across the lot.

"Is that a Dodge Charger?" Kyra called after hm, admiring his sporty red ride.

He smiled over his shoulder. "Yeah. My wife calls it my mid-life crisis vehicle!"

As Kyra sank into her own plain sedan she chuckled to herself. Between Simon's Corvette, Principal Vaughan's Charger, and another sporty blue car she'd seen in the teacher's lot a few times but had not taken the time to really look at, her sedan was looking pretty mundane. If she was going to work at this school she just might have to upgrade her wheels.

Chapter 6

The first full week of school was over! A week and a half down. Kyra leaned back in her desk chair and stretched her arms over her head as the last of the bustle and shouting in the hallway subsided. She'd made it! Now hopefully she could get the rest of her unpacking done this weekend. She'd purposely not handed out homework these last few days so that she wouldn't have anything to grade this weekend. And she didn't even feel mildly guilty about that.

She'd made good use of her preparation period over the last couple days and had all her lessons for the next two weeks laid out. The kids had loved the break she'd given them to write up scripts and perform them in class. And she had seen a renewed interest in the subject, which thrilled her to no end. Now, she just needed to get her newly-arrived chart "The Anatomy of a Castle" and some other Medieval paraphernalia pinned to the bulletin board, so that next week when they continued their discussions of works from the middle ages, the kids would have better visuals to look at. And then she could go home, slip into a pair of comfortable sweats, finish unpacking, and hopefully sleep in as late as possible tomorrow.

Outside her door the hallways had fallen quiet. Most of the kids must have headed home.

She slipped off her shoes and hefted her tub of bulletin board items, but just then there was a knock on her door and a brunette poked her head inside.

Drat, one more interruption that was going to delay her departure.

But it always paid to be friendly so Kyra smiled at her, recognizing her as one of the other teachers who had attended this morning's staff meeting. The meeting had gone long, however, and everyone had needed to rush off for their classrooms, so Kyra hadn't really gotten to meet anyone. It touched her that the woman had chosen to come by.

"We made it to Friday," she offered the woman a fist-pump of greeting.

The brunette stepped more fully into the classroom. "We did. First full week down." She stretched her hand out to Kyra. "I'm Ashley Adams. I'm sorry I haven't had time to come meet you till now. Things have been a little hectic, and with you taking your lunches at home..." She left the sentence to trail and Kyra wasn't sure if there was censure in her tone or just mild curiosity.

She decided to give the woman the benefit of the doubt. She balanced her tub on one hip and squeezed the woman's hand. "I'm Kyra Radell. Nice to meet you. I only moved to the island last Monday, so I've been taking my lunch breaks at home to do a little unpacking. Hopefully, I'll be able to get that done this weekend. What do you teach?"

Ashley folded her arms and pulled a face. "You mean what do I attempt to teach, right?"

Kyra wasn't sure how to respond to that.

But if Ashley noticed it didn't seem to faze her. She waved a hand and pressed on. "Kids these days have no respect." She blinked and then smiled a bit sheepishly. "Sorry. It's been a rough start to the year. I teach freshman and sophomore math. I've already had to send three students to the office and it's only been a week and a half of school." She sighed and collapsed into one of the desks, angling herself to face the bulletin board Kyra had stepped over to. "So, you're new to the island, huh? Where did you move here from?"

Kyra pinned her old-world map of Europe to the top right corner of the bulletin board. Maybe she could work and talk and not be delayed in getting home at all. "Just across the sound. From Everett. Have you lived here all your life?"

"Born and raised. I went to school at Western in Bellingham. Other than that, my life has pretty much consisted of islands and waves and seagulls."

There was an edge of bitterness to her tone that Kyra didn't really understand. "Not a bad way to live, right?"

Ashley hummed a thoughtful note. "I guess. I shouldn't complain."

The room fell quiet for a few minutes, and Kyra felt the tension of silence between strangers. She filled it with, "How long have you worked here at Cedar Harbor High?"

"Just over fifteen years now."

"Wow, that would put you at what? Almost forty? I never would have pegged you there. You age really well." The words were out before Kyra thought better of them. She scrunched up her nose. "Sorry. I'm forever putting my foot in my mouth."

Ashley chuckled. "I'll take compliments like that anytime. And if I have had a few tucks and lifts here and there, well, that will be our little secret." She smiled.

Kyra decided she liked the woman.

Ashley unfolded herself from the desk chair. "So I really came by to see if you wanted to join me for dinner tonight? The Harbor House has delicious steak and seafood. My treat?"

Kyra suppressed a groan. So much for just being able to hide away at home this evening and getting her new little house in order. But it would seem rude to turn the woman down. And she had to eat, right? "Sure. What time?"

Ashley looked at her watch. "What if we say five thirty?"

Kyra forced a smile. She really was grateful for the offer of friendship. She would cling to that. "Five thirty it is. I'll meet you there. And thank you."

Kyra pulled her car into a parking space at the Harbor House just a few minutes early.

As she slung her purse over her shoulder, a middle-aged man was getting out of the car next to hers. And from the passenger seat—

Kyra froze as Case Sheridan stepped from the car. Honestly, it just wasn't fair that the kid was so handsome and...manly.

He blinked at her. "Uh, hello Miss Radell." Was his face flushing? Probably hoping beyond hope that she didn't rat him out to his father. Sure enough, the kid tossed a glance at the man who was looking between them with a speculative squint to his eyes. Probably in his early fifties, the man was balding, but his angular features were bronzed and chiseled and he had a pair of the prettiest gray-green eyes she'd seen in a long while—probably where Case got his stunning eyes from. Women Mr. Sheridan's age would probably call him handsome.

"Case, use your manners," the man snapped.

Kyra felt her face flush a little. Had she been staring?

"Oh." Case cleared his throat. "Dad, this is Miss Radell. She teaches me English and PE. Miss Radell, this is my dad, Mick Sheridan. He works in insurance."

Mr. Sheridan stepped toward her and held out his hand. "It's a pleasure to meet you, Miss Radell. I trust my son has been on his best behavior these first few days of school?"

Kyra bit her lip. She hated her first impression to be that of a teacher tattling on her student. So she only smiled and turned a question back on him. "Case tells me you two are new to the area?"

The man nodded. "Just moved here, yes. But I'm not sure I like how you are avoiding my question, Miss Radell." He chuckled, but glowered good-naturedly at his son.

Case's foot kicked at the ground.

Kyra searched for a reply that would be both honest and conciliatory. She didn't want to get the boy into too much trouble. She settled for, "To be honest, he has been late a couple times, but I'm sure settling into a new school in his senior year of high school has to be difficult. He'll get the schedule figured out soon enough."

Mr. Sheridan gave her a squint.

Kyra gasped as she realized the man could take her words as an insult. "Not that I'm saying your moving here was wrong. I'm certain there was no help for it." She bounced a glance between the two.

Case was still intent on the ground beneath his feet. And Mr. Sheridan was now a bit less pinch-lipped. Still, she would do better to end this conversation sooner than later.

Ashley's arrival was the interruption she needed. She parked across the lot and down a few spaces.

"If you'll excuse me?" Kyra stepped toward Ashley's car. "It truly has been a pleasure to meet you, but the person I'm meeting just arrived. Have a good evening."

As she made her escape, she pondered on the fact that, other than exquisite eyes, Case really didn't look much like his father. He must take after his mother's side of the family. She wondered what had happened to the woman?

Case and Captain Danielson watched her hurry away.

The captain turned to him and spoke low. "She didn't throw you under the bus. Do you think she knows you aren't really who you say you are?"

With a sinking sensation in the pit of his stomach, Case watched her until she disappeared through the doors of the restaurant with Ashley Adams before he answered the question. "No. She believes us. She thinks I'm a kid who was playing at being a grown up last Saturday."

"How do you know?"

Case gave a longsuffering sigh. "Because she no longer looks at me like a woman who is attracted to a man."

Mick whistled sympathetically, then clapped him on the shoulder. "The things we give up for this job, huh? But come on. We need to get inside. I'm told that this place has great food in addition to being the center of a lot of the Friday night action in this small town. If someone is selling drugs on this island, this is the place to start our search."

Case followed after him but not until he groused good-naturedly, "You owe me a raise and an extra week of vacation pay every year."

The captain only laughed.

Just as Mick had predicted, the inside of the restaurant bustled with activity. A sign just inside the door and in front of the hostess stand read "Please wait to be seated." Beyond the hostess stand, most of the tables in the restaurant were visible.

While they waited, Case took the opportunity to study the room. Kyra—*Miss Radell*, he silently corrected himself—had taken a seat at a table with Miss Adams. He didn't have the woman for any classes, but he made a mental note that they should look into her more.

At a table further back, Mr. Hall sat with a myriad of papers spread out all around him. A thick book also sat on the table beside him. He was either grading papers or creating lesson plans. From this distance it was hard to know. What he could see, however, was the interest that registered in the man's eyes when he lifted his gaze and took note of Kyra.

Case gritted his teeth and continued his perusal.

Across the room from Mr. Hall, Principal Vaughan sat at a table having dinner with a woman, likely his wife. The woman appeared to be at least fifteen years the man's junior. But that could be from having some work done? He couldn't quite tell from here. Either way it was interesting. Even more interesting was the fact that Vaughan seemed to be pleading with her about something. The man reached across the table to touch her hand, but she pulled away with a shake of her head and a few low words. Trouble on the home front? Maybe. One more thing to check into at least.

Two police officers sat at the table adjacent to the Vaughans. Case's stomach tightened. A rookie cop had once almost given away his op and ever since then he'd been a bit leery of what officers might do, especially in a situation like this where the men knew both he and Mick were under. Their first day on the island they'd had a quiet meeting with all three of the officers on the island. In a small community like Cedar Harbor, where everyone seemed to know everyone's business, they'd needed to keep the meeting quiet, so they'd arranged to meet after dark at the house they were renting. The officers had walked over from the precinct and come through the backyard. Hopefully, none of their neighbors were the observant nosy types who saw everything that went on in the neighborhood. So far none of their neighbors had broached the subject with them, so Case thought they'd probably gone unobserved. At any rate, today neither officer gave them more than a cursory glance, and Case gave them props for keeping their cool.

Other than the four teachers and the officers, several families sat throughout the room, but Case only saw two kids from the high school. One was Chloe Schumacher. He groaned inwardly as she smiled her sultry smile at him from across the room. He gave her a nod and what he hoped was a smile that indicated interest but not commitment. The other student was Ramon Diaz, or RD, as the kids at school called him. He was one of the boys who had been ogling Miss Radell that first day of PE class and Case was working on getting into the kid's circle of friends. He had a feeling that Ramon was a kid to keep an eye on. Case also gave him a casual nod of greeting and Ramon returned the greeting with a hand gesture that looked like a W with his two middle fingers slightly crossed to form the center of the letter and his first finger and pinky forming the outside. Case had seen the gesture around school a few times. He made a note to mention it to Mick and to try and find out more about it at school next week. A gang sign? Out here in this small community? Maybe.

The hostess came and escorted them to a table. Mick gave the menu a cursory glance before setting it aside. Case knew he would order the BLT. The man could live on those things.

Mick leaned in to the table and kept his voice low. "So, any updates? You seen anything suspicious at the school? Heard any scuttlebutt?"

Case almost grinned at the man's old navy term, but remembered just in time that he was supposed to be a sullen teenager. People might not be able to hear them over the music streaming from the restaurant speakers and the conversations of the other tables, but they were certainly watching them— the new people in town.

Case shook his head. "No. Haven't had time to get close to any of the kids yet. But I have a couple of promising irons in the fire." Deciding on the steak and garlic mashed potatoes with grilled asparagus, he set his menu aside. "I hear there's supposed to be a party next Friday night. I'm working on getting myself an invite."

The waitress returned and took their orders. Sure enough,

Mick ordered a BLT and sweet iced tea. Case chose a Coke and asked for his steak to be medium rare.

He tried not to be distracted by the fact that he had a perfect line of sight to Kyra Radell, especially since he'd gotten an idea the moment he'd seen that Ramon was in the restaurant. He felt certain that Ramon was a kid who would know things, but it took some foundational groundwork to break into a tight-knit group of friends. And Ramon and his group were definitely tight-knit.

He waited till the waitress left, then leaned across the table to speak low to Mick. "So... I have an idea. Kid at the table at three o'clock is someone I'm trying to get in with. What do you say I throw a big teenage fit and walk out on you tonight?"

Mick's brow's lifted. "If you feel it will help you with your work."

Case bit back a smile, forcing himself to instead fold his arms and look sullen. "I think it will. I'm hoping he'll offer me a ride. But not before I finish my steak."

Mick looked like he wished he could chuckle. "And what if he starts to leave early?"

Case groaned. "You better ask for a box and bring my meal to the house then. I'm starving."

"Alright. What is our argument going to be about?"

Case pondered on that. Ramon was athletic. He'd seen the kid heading to soccer practice a few times. And Case didn't think Ramon had seen too much of his "klutziness" on the tennis courts during PE. If he was going to get in with the kid, he might need to rethink his strategy in that area. "I think it should be about the fact that I want to try out for the soccer team, but you won't let me."

Mick nodded. "Alright. I can roll with that. A kid just sat down at Mr. Hall's table. Do you recognize him?"

Case gave a casual glance over his shoulder. He recognized

the teen, but hadn't yet learned his full name. He turned back to Mick. "He's in my senior English class. He goes by the name Greg, but it might be short for Gregory and I haven't caught a last name yet. Studious type though. Always quick with the answers and generally right. Strikes me as someone who can't handle being told that he's wrong."

Mick pondered, studying the teacher and boy for a moment. "Tutoring?"

Case smirked. "You mean is he tutoring Mr. Hall?"

Mick gave him a "be serious" look.

"Sorry. Kidding of course. I mean, maybe he's there for tutoring. But my bet would be no. You got your camera on?" Each of them had a small camera on their person. The captain's was in one of the buttons on his shirt. Case's was in the arrowhead pendant that hung from the leather strap around his neck.

Mick gave him another glance that said, "do you really need to ask?"

That was good. They could analyze the footage more closely later. While they waited for their food, Mick gave him a play-by-play of what was happening at the table. "Greg just handed Hall a folder. Hall is looking at some papers inside. Now he's pulled something out of his briefcase. I can't tell what it is. But he put it into the folder and handed it back to the kid. It's not a paper, because the folder isn't closing all the way."

Case tried not to be distracted by Kyra's low chuckle over something Ashley Adams had just said. How ironic that the first woman he'd been interested in for a long time had suddenly fallen onto the "off limits" list. He sighed.

Mick suddenly raised his voice just a notch too loud. "I'm telling you your schoolwork has to come first. So the answer is no."

Case came back to attention just in time to see Chloe heading their way.

Greg stood from Hall's table, and the two crashed into each other.

"Oh! I'm so sorry!" Chloe said.

But her eyes rolled when Greg scrambled to gather the contents of his folder. Chloe bent to help him, beating him to the folder. She tucked a few things inside and handed it back to him.

"Thanks," Greg muttered and hurried into the restaurant bathroom.

Case pulled his mind from logging the details of their encounter and reminded himself to get back into character. "Dad I can keep up with the work *and* play soccer!"

Several heads in the restaurant turned their way, including Miss Radell.

Chloe stopped by their table. She cast an uncertain look between them, twirling one long blonde lock. "Uh, maybe this isn't a good time?"

Case focused his best glower on Mick. "It's fine." He switched expressions abruptly, and offered her a forced smile. "What's up?"

She shrugged one shoulder. "I was just on my way out." She gestured to the table she'd just left where two adults were still studying her with a bit of worry in their eyes. "My parents have finally cut me loose for the evening. But thought I'd come over to say hi." She cast a suddenly embarrassed glance toward Mick.

Case offered a sigh full of what he hoped sounded like teen angst. It wasn't too far from his true feelings because he suddenly realized that he wasn't going to get his steak right now. Impromptu was the name of the game undercover. And they'd made enough of a scene that word would get around in a small town like this. He could leave with Chloe right now and maybe engender himself some points with RD for thinking quick on his feet when a pretty girl was around.

Fixing his gaze on Chloe, he tossed down his napkin and stood. "You want to get out of here?"

Chloe looked surprised.

He couldn't blame her because he'd done his best all week to put her off.

She blinked. "Uh sure."

"Great. Let's go." He swept past her and started from the room.

Chloe's heels clicked as she followed him.

Behind them, he heard the scrape of Mick's chair. "Case Presley Sheridan, you get back here right now! You haven't even eaten yet!"

At the use of the middle name assigned to his cover, it was almost more than he could do to keep his grumpy expression. The King had been Mick's idol when he was a teen even though Elvis's reign had been well before his time. The whole unit had given the captain a hard time for sneaking in a use of his name on this op.

Case tossed a wave over his shoulder. "I'm not hungry." And with that, he banged through the door and left Mick to deal with the aftermath of their disagreement.

CHAPTER 7

Keeping a straight face was difficult as the new kid banged out into the parking lot of the Harbor House. Laughing while everyone in the room gave each other shocked looks or tossed the father sympathetic ones would probably not go over too well.

But... *Drama much?* The kid obviously needed to chill out a little. Maybe some Fire was in order. That ought to relax him and take the edge off. The smirk did slip free then, but only for the briefest of moments. Hopefully, the quick swipe of the napkin hid the expression from others. The fleeting reminder that in this business one had to be very careful who they approached to sell their product to also came to mind.

A sigh slipped free. Making money selling drugs definitely had its challenges.

Connie, the waitress, showed up just then with the Sheridans' plates.

The dad—was his name Mick?—waved a hand to the boy's meal. "I'll need a box for that one, it seems."

Connie smiled placatingly. "No problem. Do you want me to keep it in the warmer till you leave?"

Did my eyes just roll? Selling drugs might be more dangerous than waiting tables, but it likely required a lot less patience.

The dad shook his head. "No need for that. Thanks."

The chatter in the room slowly resumed as everyone turned back to their own meals.

Greg Salazar exited the bathroom and started outside. That was the cue. They were supposed to meet out by Greg's car in just a few moments now, but the transaction would have to be delayed. With Case and Chloe out there, right now was too risky. But Greg would wait. After only two sales the kid was so hooked there was no need to worry that he'd drive away without buying. The hungry eyes that flicked this way even now, revealed that much.

A subtle shake of the head hopefully registered with the kid that it would be a few minutes yet.

A few more sips of water. A few more bites of the salad that had been pushed aside earlier. An order of the Harbor House specialty dessert—caramel ice cream swirled with chocolate fudge. And, annoyingly, a bit more conversation was necessary.

But finally, the moment for goodbyes arrived.

It didn't take more than an "accidental" bump into Greg in the dusk-cloaked, empty parking lot to swap a little bag of Fire for cold hard cash. And the deed was done.

Spirits buoyed as the soft leather of the sports car's seat welcomed.

It was done.

And so much easier than waiting tables.

A knock on his door woke Case at three thirty AM. He pushed himself up to one elbow, rubbing his eyes with thumb and forefinger. "Yeah?"

Mick poked his head through the door. "Sheriff just called. They've got another body."

Case came wide awake. "I'll be right out."

Mick nodded and withdrew.

Case pulled on jeans and thrust his arms through the sleeves of a T-shirt as he pushed through his door and headed toward the living room. Mick was just pressing the "brew" button on the coffee pot.

Case pulled two mugs from the cupboard and set them on the counter, then leaned against it and folded his arms. Of course, to keep their cover they would need to stay away from the scene of the crime, but maybe the police had been more helpful than usual with some information. "They say who it is? And know for sure it was an OD?"

The bags under Mick's eyes proved that he wasn't quite awake yet either. "They only found the body fifteen minutes ago, so COD isn't confirmed. But the kid's name is Greggory Salazar. Pictures should be coming through soon. So I haven't seen him yet. But you said the kid sitting at Hall's table last night was named Greg. Same kid?"

Case stepped over to the stacks of student files that covered the dining table and fingered through to the S section. "Salazar...Salazar. Here it is." He tugged it out and flipped it open. His heart sank. "Yeah, it's him." He handed the folder over to Mick.

Enough coffee had dripped into the carafe for two cups, so while Mick perused the file, Case filled their cups. He nudged one cup toward Mick, put the carafe back under the spout, and then took a hearty sip from his own cup.

Mick slammed the folder onto the top of the stacks with one palm, coffee going unnoticed. "This kid was only seventeen years old!" He cursed.

Case held his silence. This was the hardest part of their job. The kid's death had happened on their watch. That never felt good. In fact, it felt way too much like failure. *His* failure. Could he have figured this out sooner? Worked faster? Dug deeper? Maybe even befriended Greg and prevented him from taking the drugs altogether? That was the problem with this job. Evil struck from all directions and it wasn't humanly possible to be looking everywhere at once. He pulled in a breath and gritted his teeth against the wash of anger that threatened to roll over him. He'd learned long ago not to give in to the anger. It only caused him to make mistakes, and right now they couldn't afford any more of those.

Instead he turned all the pent-up emotions toward prayer. *God, it would be really great if You could help us catch this guy before any other kids are killed.*

Mick's phone buzzed. He grunted. "Pictures are here."

They stepped into the living room and Mick paired his phone to the large screen hanging on one wall.

Case felt a chill grip him. The first picture was of the victim behind the wheel of his car. And in the background… "Is that Harbor House?"

Mick looked grim.

"So did he never leave the parking lot?"

Mick rubbed the back of his neck and then texted back to the officer who had sent him the images. "I'll ask about surveillance footage." Only a moment later he grunted in satisfaction. "He said they'll send it our way as soon as they get it."

Case sighed, swiping the screen to see the images of the victim and his car from the other angles. "At least the restaurant has cameras. I wasn't certain they would." He tapped on a zoomed-in image. "What's this?"

There was a tiny ziplock bag filled with orange crystals in the image.

Mick took a closer look. "Is that this new drug?"

Case tapped the image again. "We should make sure they fingerprint that. Inside and out. And give us an analysis as soon as they have it."

"Already on it." Mick fired off a text.

The next hour was spent carefully analyzing all the images

and reading Greggory Salazar's file from cover to cover. There didn't seem to be any signs of a struggle—and that assessment came from both the images and the officers who were actually able to view the body at the crime scene. From all the evidence this appeared to be another overdose.

It was nearly five AM when the email with the link to download the security footage arrived. Careful assessment showed Greg arriving at the restaurant just after they had around five thirty the evening before. But he'd parked in the back corner of the lot where the cameras didn't reach. Still, there were no other exits from the parking lot, and his car had never left the lot. If he'd spoken to anyone other than Mr. Hall and Chloe inside the restaurant, it wasn't visible on the footage.

Mick and Case sat back in their chairs and looked at each other.

Mick swallowed the last of his third cup of coffee and started another pot. "Alright, we know the kid never left the lot after he arrived. He spoke to Hall. And to Chloe, briefly. And we don't know if he spoke to anyone else by his vehicle. Where does that leave us?"

Case leaned back in his chair and clasped his hands behind his head. "Either he had the drugs on him when he arrived. Or one of the people who was in that restaurant is our dealer. Or someone came into the parking lot from an angle we can't see with the cameras and sold him the drugs."

Mick pulled up the still images of the crime scene again. He enlarged one and pointed to the background. "Unless our dealer is in the habit of hopping—what would you say? A nine-foot fence?—it's not likely that he came into the lot from the back."

Case nodded. "Good catch." The fence in the image was high and covered with an overgrowth of vines that didn't appear to be disturbed. "Ask them if there's any evidence of someone having climbed the fence. Broken vines? Fresh leaves on the ground? If not, I say we concentrate on the people who were eating there last night. Chances are slim that the kid would arrive with the drugs, go in to talk to Hall, and then OD in the parking lot before going home. If he was that desperate to get the drugs in his system, doesn't it seem probable that he would have shot up the moment he got his hands on them?"

Mick nodded.

"To me that says he either bought them in the restaurant, or from someone outside afterward."

Mick nodded again. "I agree."

"Think Chloe could have slipped them to him?"

Mick pondered. "From all appearances, that little crash they had was totally accidental. I think she was intent only on coming over to see you. Did she act strange while you were out walking?"

Case shook his head. "Not really."

Mick considered for a few more moments. "Well we can't rule her out. But I'm thinking she's low on our priority list."

Case nodded his agreement and glanced at his watch. "I need to get in the shower if I'm going to make it to the school in time for my Saturday morning detention." He ignored Mick's smirk. "But I think the cops should have a chat with Simon Hall about what might have been in that folder we saw him hand to Greg last night. Two officers were in the dining room too, so they can pass it off as if they were the ones who saw the exchange."

"Right." Mick stood and clapped him on the shoulder. "Happy detention-ing. I'll get on this other stuff and hopefully have an update for you when you get home this afternoon. And son..." He paused for dramatic effect. "Please be on your best behavior at school today."

The news had already reached the community. Case knew it the moment he walked into detention. The supervising teacher hadn't arrived yet and all the students were talking a hundred miles an hour. All of them except RD, who was the reason Case had contrived to get himself assigned to detention in the first place. RD had his arms folded against his desk and was simply taking in all the conversation around him with a slight smirk on his face.

Case plunked himself into the empty desk next to RD and leaned close to him. "What's got everyone so upset?"

RD greeted him with a gesture of his signature W before he shrugged. "Kid named Salazar went out in a ball of Fire last night, yo."

All around them snickers broke out.

Case pretended ignorance. "He have a car crash or something?"

RD looked at him. "No man. He was at the double H for about a dime. Next thing we all know, cops found him eyes to the sky in his ride."

So not only had word spread, but it was all fairly accurate too. Case considered the way RD had emphasized the word "fire."

RD's eyes narrowed. He leaned close and lowered his voice as the chatter around them rose once more. "Saw you leave just before he died. You dealing the Fire? I hear it's some good stuff, man."

This time there was no mistaking the name Fire. That must be the street name for the orange crystals the police had found in the victim's car.

Was he really asking for a drug that he knew had likely killed a kid last night? Or just trying to get more information?

Or was RD the cook and mastermind behind the drug and simply trying to get the word out?

No matter the scenario, Case wanted to dress the kid down and back up again. Instead, he reminded himself that he'd once been a stupid teenager too, and only shook his head. "Wasn't me, man. But if you figure out where to score some, let me in on the secret, yeah?"

Case clenched his jaw. If only Chloe hadn't insisted that they walk down to the beach last night, he might have been in the parking lot to see what had gone down. Either that, or seeing him there might have scared the dealer off and it would have saved Greg's life.

Mr. Carter, the study hall teacher, walked in before RD could respond, but Case was satisfied with the next step he'd taken to befriend the kid.

Now it remained to be determined if RD was putting on an act or if he truly was innocent of the distribution of the drug called Fire.

Kyra felt like she'd been run over by a train on Monday morning when she got to school and heard the news. She'd only had Greg Salazar in her class for a week and a half, but he'd been a quiet, polite kid. She'd had no idea he was doing drugs. Should she have seen any signs? Was his death her fault?

A special assembly of the student body had been called, which was just as well because the students in her first-period class were silent and withdrawn. They needed the time with the special counselors, and the release to process the news with their friends. If the death had happened on school property during school hours the school probably would have been shut down for several days, but since it had happened on the weekend and off campus, it had been decided to keep the kids' routines as uniform as possible.

The week passed with a lot of shed tears and a school memorial assembly for Greg on Thursday morning. Many of the kids in this small community had known Greg their entire lives.

The police had been on campus several times, asking the kids questions, but as far as Kyra knew they hadn't figured out where Greg got the drugs yet. The police had even questioned her and Ashley and Simon and Principal Vaughan since they'd all been at the restaurant that night. Kyra wished she had something more to give them, but the truth was, she'd been so intent on ignoring one Case Sheridan that night, that she'd hardly paid attention to anyone else in the room. Of course, she hadn't told the police *that*.

Case had been interviewed too. An officer had come and removed him from class on Tuesday morning. But there had been something about the casual matter-of-fact way that he'd faced the interview that had piqued her attention.

Something wasn't right about that kid. The first few days of tennis, he'd acted like he had two left feet. Then suddenly on Monday morning, he'd come to class and seemed like a totally different kid.

And on this gloriously sunny day that had made her oh so happy to take her class out to the tennis courts, she had witnessed more of the same. The kid, who last week could barely connect with the ball, had slammed down several aces today. Kyra was still speculating about his rapid transition when she glanced at her watch and noticed the period was over. She blew her whistle and let the kids head back into the gym to change their clothes. She watched Case's lean athletic jog from behind and shook her head.

Simon Hall was the school's soccer coach. He'd mentioned

to her in the teachers' lounge yesterday that he'd tried to talk Case into coming out for the team, but that the kid had said his father had forbidden it so that he would keep his grades up. Yet with most kids as athletic as Case, joining a sport was often the incentive they needed to keep their grades up. Maybe she should have a talk with his father. It was obvious that the kid needed some extra motivation. And yet, from their meeting on Friday evening, she just couldn't see Case's father welcoming her input.

Kyra pushed into her office and dropped her whistle into her desk drawer. There was definitely something...intriguing about that family. Yet didn't every family have their own unique quirks? So why was she so interested in this one?

She rolled her eyes at herself. *Like you don't know.*

For the rest of the week she kept an eye on Case, trying to decide what to do. She didn't want him—or any of the kids, for that matter—to be the next victim of this latest drug. Chloe Schumacher was obviously interested in him, but he kept her at a careful arm's length. Twice Kyra had to wake Case up in the middle of English class, but each time she got the feeling that he was putting on an act when he "woke up." Twice more he was late for English, and another time he was late to PE. Yet his answers in the discussion they were having in English about Chaucer's *Canterbury Tales*, when she pinned him down for them, seemed well thought out, and mature beyond his years just as they had been in the discussion about Beowulf. But today he'd been late for first period again, and she couldn't let that slide. So when the bell rang for dismissal and everyone rose to leave, Kyra called Case's name. "Case? Hang around a minute, will you?"

He didn't look happy about it, but he dipped his head and sauntered toward her desk, backpack slung over one shoulder, while the other students filed from the room. Chloe gave Case a sympathetic smile on her way out the door and tossed a glower at Kyra for good measure.

Kyra took in a slow breath to ease the nervous jitters that suddenly swept through her. Confrontation was not her strong suit. And that was complicated by the undeniable truth that she'd been massively attracted to him when he'd been in the salon that day.

Case stopped before her desk and lifted his brows to question why she'd detained him.

Feeling at a distinct disadvantage, sitting as she was, she stood. "Case listen, I know you are new to the area and especially since you transferred in as a senior that can mean some turmoil with getting settled. But it's the third week of school and I'm beginning to see a pattern of tardiness. And there's also the sleeping in class." She pegged him with what she hoped came across as a stern but compassionate look. "Is there anything troubling you at home? Or something I should be aware of? I'm happy to work with you in any way I can."

He shuffled his feet and hooked one thumb into the strap of his backpack.

She felt chagrinned when his action drew her gaze to his chiseled bicep and quickly swept her focus back to his face.

He shook his head. "No ma'am. I'll try and do better."

"Are you getting enough sleep?"

He cast a longing glance toward the exit and scrubbed at the back of his neck. "Yeah."

Kyra folded her arms, not sure what else she should say. This was his first warning, so she supposed she'd said enough for now. "Okay, in the future please do your best to be on time, and I won't tolerate sleeping in my class."

He dipped his chin in a nod and started for the door.

She had a sudden question and spoke before she thought

better of it. "Case? You haven't heard anything about this new drug, have you?"

He froze with his back to her for a long moment, and then slowly turned to face her. His features seemed a little pale, but he said, "No. I haven't heard anything."

Kyra narrowed her eyes. "Your expression tells me otherwise."

He shook his head. "No, ma'am. I just think maybe you should leave the investigating up to the police. I'd hate to see something happen to you."

Kyra felt a chill slip down her spine. She stiffened. "Was that a threat?"

Case's eyes widened. "No, ma'am! I didn't mean it like that."

She relaxed a little. "Well, alright then. I hope you'll let me know if you do hear anything. And I'll be sure to go straight to the police with it. Alright?"

He gripped the back of his neck and said, "Yes, ma'am."

But she had the feeling that she'd likely be the last person he'd tell if he really did know something. Yet now that the idea had claimed her, she couldn't seem to let it go. "Tell you what..." She held out one hand to stop his retreat once again. "If you do learn something you can let me know anonymously. Just leave a note anytime in my inbox." She motioned to the metal compartment on her wall where she had students turn in their papers and assignments. "And you can help me spread the word about that to the students I don't have in classes too, alright?"

Case looked like he was about to say something else, but just then Simon Hall stepped through her classroom door. He looked nicely put together with a cornflower-blue shirt and matching tie. Noting that she was with a student, he motioned to her that he would wait by the door.

Kyra smiled at him and then returned her focus and a serious expression to Case. "Thank you for staying. You're free to go. Please spread the word, and do let me know if there is any way I can help to make your transition to this school easier."

Case looked back and forth between her and Simon, before he said, "Thanks," and made his way toward the door.

Kyra loosed a sigh of satisfaction. It was nice to have finally thought of a way that she might be able to help with the drug situation. Her helplessness to fix the problem had been plaguing her all week. But this was a tangible way she could help and it might garner some leads for the police. She would make the announcement to all her classes for the rest of the day.

Kyra smiled at Simon, then bent to straighten some papers on her desk. "What can I do for you?"

Chapter 8

Case was thankful to see that the hallway outside Kyra's classroom was empty. He'd be late for second period, but he had more important things to attend to at the moment. He leaned back against the wall, his heart thundering a hundred miles an hour. She was going to get herself into deep water trying to put herself into the middle of an investigation. If she learned something she wasn't supposed to and the dealer found out about it? There was no telling what might happen to her. But how to convince her to let it go? That he'd have to ponder on.

As for her accusations...

The truth was, he'd been late to first period several times because he'd been stopping at the empty lot behind the school where kids hung out to take a smoke before heading into classes. So far he hadn't seen anyone doing drugs, but he figured that group of kids was probably the best place to start hunting down information—and Chloe Schumacher had been happy to introduce him to everyone. Case doubted that Chloe's preacher daddy—something he'd recently learned about her—would appreciate learning where his daughter spent the bulk of her mornings before school.

As for Miss Radell's second charge, he'd never fallen asleep in her class. But a little snoozing act went a long way to fostering the reputation he wanted to create for himself. Kids tended to open up more when he passed himself off as just a little bit of a ne'er-do-well.

And right now, fostering that reputation coincided nicely with his need to learn a little more about Simon Hall. The police had picked him up for questioning in the death of Greg early last Saturday, but he'd said that Greg had asked him for help on a chemistry assignment and that their meeting at the restaurant had been about that. The bulky folder that Simon had handed the kid had been in the passenger seat of Greg's car when they'd found his body, and it turned out that the folder had a thumb drive inside that contained instructions and video examples for the assignment. Simon had been released and cleared of suspicion.

But Case hadn't been able to shake his doubts. Couldn't the drugs have been handed to Greg at the same time as the folder? He'd hoped that the baggie of drugs would have some fingerprints on it, but unfortunately, it had come back clean, inside and out, which was another thing in Simon's favor since he had not been wearing gloves that night at the restaurant. If he'd touched the baggie, his fingerprints would have been on it. Not that there weren't ways around that.

But, at any rate, Case wanted to hear what the chemistry teacher had to say to Miss Radell. And if that had even more to do with personal curiosity than any premonitions he had about Simon's potential as a drug dealer, well, he could still justify it as work. Had Simon overheard Kyra's plan to offer kids a way to anonymously let her know if they learned anything about the drugs? How long had the man been at the door before they'd noticed him?

Case gritted his teeth. Maybe he needed to have one of the officers come and tell her what a bad idea it was for her to get involved.

A sound from inside the room drew him back to the

present. He eased closer to the opening and strained to hear the conversation happening in the room he'd just left.

Simon's footsteps grew fainter as he obviously strode toward Kyra's desk. "It's Friday."

Case almost rolled his eyes. The guy needed a better opening line than that if he was going to win the "sworn-off-the-double-crossing-species-known-as-men" Kyra Radell.

"I know and I'm so happy about that. I finally got the last of the unpacking done the other day, but I started painting my living room and I'm hoping to finish that this weekend."

Score one for Kyra.

Despite her subtly perfected put-off, Simon pressed his luck. "But you have to eat at some point, right? Let me take you to dinner tonight? There's this great fish and chips bar, right down near the water. It gets great views of the sunset and the food is good too."

Kyra tapped some papers on her desk and Case heard her heels click against the tiles and the swish of the white-board eraser she must be putting to use. "That sounds lovely, but I'm not sure that we should be going to dinner with each other, especially since we work together."

"Oh!" Simon did his best to sound shocked. "I'm so sorry. I didn't—I was just asking you out as one colleague to another. My way of welcoming you to the team, so to speak. I didn't mean—Sorry if it came across differently."

Case twisted his lips. Yeah right.

"Well then, let's make it a group thing. How about we bring along Ashley and Darcy and Dave, as well? We can all pay for ourselves."

Case grinned. Kyra Radell was no dummy.

"S-sure. That sounds great. What time works for you?"

"Say...six? Can you check with the others and let me know if the time changes?"

"Perfect. I'll do that." Simon's shoes snapped against the tiles in a rapid-fire aim for the door.

Case scrambled for a hiding place. The women's bathroom door was the closest one, and he'd been standing here for a good five minutes so it was certain no one was in there. He pushed through, and the door slipped shut just as he heard Simon's steps move past in the hallway.

He heard another sound then—one that he hadn't paid attention to in his haste to escape being seen by Simon Hall— the click of high heels on tile. And getting closer by the second. The door was already pushing in!

He leapt over to press his back against the wall where he would be hidden for a brief moment when the door was fully open. There was a privacy wall and if she just walked around that without noticing him, he'd hopefully be able to make his escape.

But his luck was running a little thin today. Kyra pushed into the room, but as the door started to shut, she must have noticed him from the corner of her eye. Eyes widening, she swung around to look his way, and gave a half-gasp-half-screech in the process.

Great. Now what was he going to do?

"Case Sheridan what are you doing in here?!" Her tone fell solidly in the camp of outraged school teacher confronting delinquent adolescent.

She took a breath and then he saw a moment of fear flash across her face and her eyes widened.

He stepped forward and put one hand on the door to keep her from yanking it open and making a run for it and potentially alerting Simon Hall to the fact that he'd been spying on them. He raised the hand he hadn't pressed to the door to show her he meant her no harm. "This is not what it looks like."

"This is exactly what it looks like! You skulking around

in the women's bathroom when you are supposed to be in second period, young man!" She gave the door a firm yank, but he kept it closed. He needed to think here. Because if she marched out there and took him down to the principal's office, and his "father" got called in, they would have to explain that he was an undercover officer and that had the potential to blow his whole cover. They had received special dispensation from the governor to come into the school without even letting the administration know about the sting, because they had no leads on who the distributor might be, and if he was part of the administration then clueing them into the investigation would render the whole operation pointless.

"Case Sheridan, you let me out of here at once. Do the right thing. The sooner you let me out, the easier it will go for you." She tugged at the door again.

"Don't be afraid. I'm not going to hurt you." He kept his voice low, so as not to scare her but took her by one arm and pulled her into the main part of the bathroom. Quickly he pushed in each stall door to make sure they were indeed alone in the room. After assuring that, he let her go, but placed himself, arms folded, between her and the exit.

He tilted his head. Considered his options. Mick had said that he could read her in if he needed to. And while he hadn't been able to eliminate any of the other teachers from his list of suspects in the last couple weeks, the one person he could say with almost one hundred percent certainty was not a drug dealer was Kyra Radell. He'd checked her out and she had just moved to the island the week school started. Before that the only record of her being on the island was on the day she'd come out for her interview several months ago.

This was his only solution. He just needed to read her in. That would also solve the problem of how to tell her to stay out of the investigation for her own safety. He could do it himself. Mick wouldn't be happy with him. Oh, not one little bit. But it was read her in or lose the entire operation. He stepped toward her but stopped when she retreated a few steps, blue eyes going dark with fear.

The quickest way to alleviate her fear was to just tell her the truth. "I have something to tell you and I need to know you can keep a secret."

She tugged at her dress jacket, and he could almost see her shoring up her courage. "Case Sheridan have you lost your mind?" She lifted a finger to admonish him. "You listen to me. We are going to walk out that door, and we are going to go down to the office, and you can tell your story to the principal. But we are not standing here for another second, do you hear me?"

She raised herself to her towering height—all of five feet four inches—and took several steps toward him, obviously hoping to cow him into moving out of her way.

He widened his stance and spread his arms to prevent her from darting around him. "I'm an undercover officer."

She stopped so suddenly she might as well have slammed into a wall.

She glanced up at him, close enough that he could see the rim of dark blue that circled her irises. She swallowed and took a step back. He could see her assessing him, thinking back to their first meeting, considering if what he was saying could be true.

Feeling an urgency to extract himself from the room, he said, "Listen, I need to get out of here before someone else comes in. But I can prove it to you. Will you at least give me till this evening? I'll come by your place with proof."

She threw up her hands and swept a gesture around the room. "What are you even doing in here?"

"Avoiding being seen by Simon Hall."

Her eyes widened. "You were spying on us?!"

He eased open the door to check the hallway and couldn't resist tossing out, "Had to see if Simon could coax some interest from you that I couldn't seem to. At least I'm not the only one you've shot down recently." The hallway was clear. He looked back at her. Gave her a quick wink. "I need your word. Give me at least until tonight?"

She remained silent, jaw slightly slack, but nodded once.

"I'll come by your place at six. And Kyra, please stay out of this investigation." He left quickly then, before she could change her mind.

He prayed she would keep her word.

Kyra collapsed back against the sinks as soon as Case left. The boy—man—had given her the fright of her life! She spun to face the mirror and studied her pale features.

Could he be blatantly lying to her? Yet hadn't she been shocked on the first day of school to learn that he was a senior in high school and not the man she'd thought him to be when they'd met at the salon? And it would certainly explain some of his odd behavior over the past couple weeks.

Her thoughts turned to another vein. They must be taking this drug situation very seriously if they'd sent an undercover cop to ferret it out. She leaned wearily in to the counter and massaged at the headache pulsing behind her temples. She supposed there was no hurt in giving him till this evening to prove himself.

But she didn't see how it could hurt to let the kids know they could anonymously give her information. She wanted to be a help, and if she learned anything she would go straight to the police.

Realization shot through her and she straightened. Case had said he was coming by at six!

Her eyes narrowed at her reflection. If he'd been listening at the door like he claimed then he had known that was the very hour she'd agreed to meet Simon and the other teachers for dinner.

Her lips pinched together in aggravation.

Lucky for Case she hadn't really been too excited about going out anyhow. But now she had to come up with an excuse to cancel! And how was Case even going to know where she lived? Her address wasn't on any paperwork because she hadn't filed anything yet.

She threw back her shoulders and arched her brows at herself. *Well, we'll just see how good of a detective this guy really is.*

And if he didn't show up and she discovered that he really was just a kid who had duped her? She eased out a breath. She'd deal with the answer to that question when the time came. But she couldn't deny that there was a great deal of relief pumping through her that her attraction toward one Case Sheridan wasn't toward a teenage boy, but toward a man. Providing he really was telling the truth.

Chapter 9

Six o'clock came and went. As well as six thirty. And Kyra was still waiting alone in her living room. She wrinkled her nose. So maybe he wasn't such a good detective, after all.

The minute she'd gotten home from school (having pled an unforeseen complication in her schedule to Simon and the other teachers) she'd set to work putting the finishing touches of paint on her living room. Why she'd cared what it might look like she couldn't quite say, but it was obvious now that all the work she'd put in would not go to impressing any police officer, undercover or otherwise, on this evening.

With a huff, she shoved herself up off the couch and headed into the kitchen to hunt through the fridge for some leftovers that might still be edible. She'd just decided that it would have to be scrambled eggs tonight, when there was a tap on the glass of the kitchen door.

With a gasp, she spun around. Case was standing on her doorstep hunched into a hoodie, and obviously going out of his way to keep his identity secret from anyone who might chance to glance into her backyard. Despite her mental remonstrations to keep this relationship professional, her pulse did a little dance as she crossed to the door.

Keeping the chain-lock in place, she cracked it open. "I was beginning to think you weren't coming. Why are you in my backyard? And how did you get through the locked gate?"

Hands shoved deeply into the pockets of a pair of Levi's, he crooked her a smile. "Doesn't do much good to lock the gate when your fence is only four feet high. I hopped it."

"How did you even find where I lived?"

He smirked. "I wouldn't be any kind of a detective if I couldn't figure that out in a small community like this."

She shook her head. "Listen, I'm not even sure I should let you in here. I'm still not even close to convinced that you are telling me the truth."

"I get that. Honestly, I do. And it's actually smart of you. But I need five minutes of your time in a fairly private place to prove to you that I am who I say I am. So do you know of a place that would make you feel more comfortable?"

Perhaps it was because he was so understanding about her trepidation, but she suddenly wasn't nearly as leery of inviting him in as she had been a moment before. She pushed the door shut, removed the chain, and then swung it wide and motioned him in. "Here is fine, but I'm warning you that I have a black belt in karate."

He grinned and lifted his palms as he slipped by her. "I'll be on my best behavior, I promise."

"You're late."

"Sorry. I had to make sure no one saw me, and Simon Hall only pulled away from the front of the house a few minutes ago.

"Simon—what?!"

Case quickly lowered the shade over the window in the door and then remained where he was with his back pressed against the wood. "Mind pulling the curtains in the living room there? And at any other windows where someone might chance to see me?"

"O-of course." Her house did have a rather open floor plan. She hurried over to oblige him. "He was really in front of my house?"

Case shifted so that his shoulder was planted into the door instead of his back. With his hip cocked out, thumbs hooked into his pockets, and the toe of one foot resting casually on the floor, he presented the most masculine of images. She swallowed and moved on to the next window.

"He didn't have binoculars, or anything. Don't worry. I think he was probably just checking to see if you'd been honest with him when you broke off your date, or if you were going to be heading out with someone else tonight." There was a subtle teasing note in the words that was now accompanied by a twinkle in his eyes.

"It wasn't a date!"

Case smirked. "Trust me. That's not the way Simon Hall saw it."

The curtains were all closed now and she stepped back into the kitchen, folded her arms, and pinned him with a look. "Listen, for all I know you are just a delinquent teen who got caught checking out the women's bathroom and came up with a crazy story. So either get to proving your claims, or plan on spending Monday morning in Mr. Vaughan's office."

Case grinned at her even as he lifted his sweatshirt to pull out the file folder tucked away there.

She caught a glimpse of washboard abs beneath a taut black T-shirt before he tugged the hoodie back into place.

He tapped the folder against one palm, his humor-filled gaze drilling into hers. "In your estimation I've gone from a would-be serial killer to a would-be delinquent..." He winked. "I'm so happy to see that I'm coming up in the world."

She snorted. "Ha ha. The next few moments will tell."

Case motioned to the loveseat visible above the half-wall of her kitchen. "Sit with me?"

She eyed the proximity of the two cushions and weighed that against the danger of her attraction to this man. Keeping her distance won out. "Actually, I was just about to make some dinner. How about you go sit at the table?" There was also a block of butcher knives right here next to her. She'd feel safer being near those.

"Sure."

He stepped across the room and sank down into a chair facing her across the table. She cracked two eggs into the pan before she thought to ask him if he was hungry.

He shrugged. "I could eat."

"Scrambled eggs with ham and cheese sound okay to you? Sorry the pickings are slim. I need to get to the store."

"Sounds good. Thanks."

Kyra cracked three more eggs into the pan and set to chopping a few slices of lunch meat.

He watched her as she worked, making her very aware of every move she made.

She needed to get this meeting rolling. If only it wasn't so hard to concentrate with him looking at her like that. She moistened her lips and tried to think where to start. "So how does an undercover agent go about proving to me that he's undercover?"

His lashes lowered languidly, and he had a hint of a smile playing around his lips that let her know her nerves probably hadn't gone unnoticed. "Well I have some paperwork here that I think will make it very clear. Barring all else you call the Everett police department and ask for Sergeant Damian Packard. He'll vouch for me."

Kyra felt like someone might pop around a corner at any moment and inform her she was on *Candid Camera*. "What is this? Some bet you took at school to see how gullible the newest teacher was?"

He sighed. "It's not like I can give you a fake number for the Everett department. You can look it up online, if you like."

She studied him for a moment. She was generally pretty good at reading people. And her instincts had been registering something off about him as a student from the first day he'd walked into her classroom.

But still... She was really torn over what to believe. She didn't want to be duped by a delinquent prankster in the first month of her first teaching gig.

His expression had lost all humor now. "Kyra, I'm not yanking your chain here. And it's really important that you believe me. So I'm going to do everything within my power to prove to you that I am who I say I am."

Kyra added slices of bread to the toaster. "Okay, what is your first piece of evidence?"

He opened the folder. "This is my driver's license."

Kyra stepped over to look at it. It looked real enough, and was under the name Case Lexington. It even had his date of birth as being two years before her own. "You are seriously twenty-five years old?"

He spread his hands and dipped a nod.

"What bands were popular when you were in school?"

He named several immediately. All of them were bands that her sister Lainey, who was also twenty-five, had raved over when they were teens. But he could have studied up on that, or simply be a music trivia buff. She fired off several more pop-culture questions from her and Lainey's time in high school. He had a satisfactory answer for every one except for her question about Natalie Portman to which he only gave her a blank look.

She arched her brows. "You don't know Natalie Portman? Padmé Amidala?"

He blinked. "From the *Star Wars* movies? Guess I never bothered to learn her name. If I'm honest, I'm not much of a *Star Wars* fan."

"I suppose I can let that one slide." She gave him a smirk as she tossed the license back on the table. "But even I know that there are places that create great looking fake IDs." The toast popped and she crossed the room to pull it out. "Butter?"

He shook his head. "No. Thanks. And come on! You think I was able to get a fake ID created between the time we spoke at school today and now?" He shook his head. "These things—especially the good ones—take more time than that."

She supposed that was true enough. But he could have had this ID made sometime in the past for some other nefarious reason. Like the weekend he'd been in Everett at the salon hitting on her. She pegged him with a look. "I do have to say that the thought crossed my mind that maybe you came into the salon that day to see if you could pass yourself off as an adult in a non-threatening environment. You could have had this for who knows how long."

He smirked. "You think I would choose a nail salon for my trial run?"

She threw up her hands. "I don't know, okay! My mind has been spinning like crazy ever since you walked into my classroom that first day." She cringed. She probably shouldn't have admitted that to him. It revealed too much emotional attachment to this. She forced her gaze back to his folder. "What else do you have for me?"

He laid another item on the table. "This is the receipt from the day I was in your sister's salon. The last four digits on it match the numbers on this credit card that is issued to... oh look at that, Case Lexington." He snapped the credit card onto the table next to the receipt before he dug into the pocket of his hoodie and said, "I also brought my badge." He dropped a heavy metal and leather badge on the table. "And here is even my passport where you can see that I went to London six weeks ago. There was a big law-enforcement conference there in the Grand Staffordshire Hotel. You can look that up too."

Kyra slid his plate in front of him, then sat down with her own and picked up the receipt and the credit card. After looking at them she examined the badge, which looked real enough, but what would she know about what a fake badge might resemble? Lastly, the passport was definitely him and the stamp for London was there just as he'd said. She did have to admit that if he was just trying to pull one over on her he was going to some extreme lengths to do it. But she was still leery of buying this proof too easily. She slid the items back across the table. "Again. They could have been printed up for you. Do you know the phone number by heart?"

He blinked. "Pardon?"

She tilted her head. "Most people know the number of the place where they work by heart."

The humor returned to his gaze. "9-1-1?"

She narrowed her eyes at him.

He lifted his hands. "Kidding. Kidding! Yes, I know the number. I can even give you a direct line to Damian's desk."

She lifted a finger. "Oh no. I won't have you giving me a number to some friend of yours who will feed me a bunch of lies. We'll go through the front switchboard and see if this Damian person even exists."

He scooped eggs onto his toast and folded the bread into a sandwich of sorts. "I can live with that." He took a huge bite.

Kyra chewed a mouthful of eggs as she tapped a search for the Everett Police department into her phone. Once she found the number she peered at him over the device. "Okay, go. What's the number?"

He chuckled. "You'd make a pretty good detective, you know that?"

She quirked one brow. "Stall much?"

He was still laughing when he rattled the number off to her without missing a single digit.

She couldn't believe how pleased she was to have him pass that little test. But she reminded herself to reserve judgment as she set the phone down. "I can't call until tomorrow, obviously. But I'll say that, for now, I guess I believe your story. So what are you over here investigating?"

He raised one brow as though to question if she really needed to ask.

"Well, of course I know it's the drugs and the kids who've died. But I just wondered if there was anything else?"

Case didn't even miss a beat. "Here's the thing. My boss about blew a gasket when I told him I was going to have to read you in. The more people who know about an op, the harder it is to keep it under wraps. So I really need to know that you will do your best not to give me away. My life could literally be in your hands."

He wasn't even going to acknowledge her questions? Did that mean there was more to this than she realized? But she wouldn't push him if he wasn't supposed to talk about it.

He kept those soft green eyes locked on her. There was so much seriousness in his expression that she felt her pulse begin to pound with fear that she might do something to blow his cover. "I'll do my best, for sure."

He nodded. "I appreciate that. And now I have a request for you."

She tilted her head, waiting for him to go on.

"Please don't ask all your students to give you anonymous information if they know anything about the drugs. It could actually put you and anyone who talks in a lot of danger."

She doodled her fork through her eggs. "But isn't that what you do? Ask a lot of questions?"

"Subtly." He raised a brow for emphasis before taking another bite. "So, what made you want to be a school teacher?"

She pinched her lips together. He was just changing the

subject like that? As if she'd agreed to his request? That grated, but maybe it was best if she dropped it for now because pressing on with that line of talk would mean she'd have to admit that she'd already spread the word to many of her students today. She could think about it over the weekend and decide what she wanted to do.

She tilted her head and savored a mouthful of ham and cheese while she pondered what to tell him of her history. She certainly didn't know him well enough yet to lay the burdensome story of her brother at his feet. She considered several variations of her history and decided on, "When I was a sophomore in high school I had a teacher who went out of his way to connect with every student every day. I had a bit of a rough year that year, but Mr. McCurry always had positive encouraging things to say no matter how badly I messed up. When I got to college and had to make a career choice, I knew I wanted to impact kids in the positive way he had influenced me." She ended with a shrug.

Case had polished off the last of his eggs and toast while she talked, and now he nodded. "From what I'm seeing at the school, I think you are doing just that." He stood. "I should be going. The less time we spend together the less chance of my cover being blown. Besides"—he grinned—"I have a party to get to." He dumped his plate into her sink and then scooped his file off the table and tucked it beneath his sweatshirt again. He shoved the badge back into his hoodie pocket. "Mind taking the trash out? Will give you an excuse to check that no one is lingering back there before I leave."

"Of course."

Kyra took out the trash. All seemed quiet, and she felt a little silly as she scrutinized every shadow or flicker of movement for several moments. The only sounds she heard were the soft swish of the waves against the shore not far away, and the soft croaking of a frog from the drainage ditch at the back of the property. Finally satisfied, she signaled Case that it was okay for him to exit the house.

"Night," was all he offered in parting.

And for some reason as he strode into the darkness and she heard him grunt softly as he vaulted her fence, nothing seemed silly anymore. The police were taking this drug situation serious enough that they'd sent in an undercover officer. Despite the warm autumn evening, fear whispered a chill down the back of her neck.

She hurried into the house and locked the door.

Chapter 10

Case didn't let himself linger on concerns for Kyra. They'd been careful and he didn't feel like he'd put her in any danger. At least not any more danger than she could be in while working at a school where someone was pushing drugs. Unless she didn't listen to his advice and tried to help in ways she shouldn't.

He hurried back to the house and stashed his badge and the paperwork in the safe. Then, after changing into clothing more appropriate to a jock at a high school party, he headed for the address that had been texted to him earlier today.

The house was a nice tri-story right on the beach with the Salish Sea splashing against the rocky shore at the far end of the backyard. Music pulsed, and teens already gyrated around the campfire that flickered from the stone pit just up from the beach. There were two coolers full of beer and a couple other bottles of harder stuff sitting on a picnic table off to one side. But right up front, nothing that looked like the orange crystals that had killed Greg Salazar.

The lab had finally sent them an update just this morning and the ingredients in this drug were scary enough to make the hair on the back of his neck stand on end as he read through the list. It was a wonder more kids hadn't died. They needed to get it out of circulation as soon as possible or they were going to have a lot more deaths on their hands.

He'd just stepped through the gate into the backyard when

Chloe bopped up to him. Her first two fingers held a half-smoked cigarette that poked out to one side, and her ponytail swayed like a California blonde. "Hey Case." She drawled his name as if it had three or four letter 'A's instead of just one.

"'Sup?" he asked.

She cocked him a funny look.

Case rubbed the back of his neck. Maybe he needed an update on teen lingo.

But after only a moment Chloe seemed to shake off her curiosity. "This is going to be a killer party. I'm glad you came." She linked her arm with his and leaned close to bat her big eyes at him.

He stifled a sigh, hoping she wouldn't literally be correct while at the same time realizing that at least one part of teen lingo hadn't changed since he was in high school. And it was time to put an end to this infatuation of hers right now. He stepped away and shoved his hands deep into his pockets, pinning his elbows to his sides so she couldn't loop her arm through his again. "Listen," he kicked at the ground not even having to fake his discomfort with this conversation, "I sort of have a girl... Back home. I mean back where I just moved from. So..."

Chloe giggled and took another drag on her cigarette. She doodled her finger across his chest blowing her smoke to the side. "What she doesn't know won't hurt her." She tilted her head coyly.

He shook his head. "I wouldn't want to treat her that way. Not the kind of guy I want to be."

"Aw, you're so sweet." She leaned close to whisper in his ear. "Which is why I'm not going to give up on you. I heard you told RD you'd like to score some Fire?" There was an innocent glimmer to her gaze that belied the danger in her question.

Case's heart thudded. Was this the breakthrough he'd been looking for? "Yeah. I heard it's some good stuff. Do you have some?"

She giggled. "Not right now. But I might be able to get you some for the right price."

"How mu—"

"Chloe Elaine Schumacher you get your butt in the car right now, young lady!"

Chloe gasped and tossed her still smoldering cigarette into the green grass behind her.

Case's eyes fell closed for a moment before he looked up to see an angry woman storming their way. Chloe's mother, whom he'd seen briefly at the restaurant. Despite his disappointment, he couldn't help but think *Good for her for tracking down her daughter like this.* But could the woman's timing be any worse?

Chloe rolled her eyes. Then with a saucy quirk of one brow, she sauntered toward her mother, hips swaying.

Case released a breath and glanced up to see RD watching him from across the yard.

Case lifted his chin in greeting.

RD returned the greeting with his W gesture.

It was time to find out what that sign was all about. He stepped over to toe out the cigarette's remaining heat, then sauntered past the cooler, snagging a cold beer as he went. He popped the tab. Not that he'd be drinking any of it, but it didn't hurt to look like he was at least trying to fit in. He ambled over to RD and was thankful when the kid greeted him and didn't force him to start up an awkward conversation.

"Yo newby. You down with my digs?" The other boys RD had been talking with quieted down and studied him with more curiosity than animosity.

Case glanced around the yard and took in the house once more, every sense on the alert. "This is your place, huh? Nice.

I like it." He reached out to shake the hands of the others in the circle. "I'm Case." Each was athletic and fit. They were probably soccer teammates of RD's. One by one they gave him their names.

"John."

"Hunter."

"Blake."

"Gerard." That name gave Case pause. Gerard Dunn was the name of one of the kids who had ODed but lived this past July. But according to Mick, the local cops had leaned on him quite heavily and he'd refused to give up his dealer. Gerard was a fairly unique name, so it likely was the same kid, but it only took Case a split second to decide that tonight was not the night to try to gather more information. He'd keep him in mind for the future.

"So what does this mean?" Case mimicked the W gesture that RD and his friends kept flaunting. "This some sort of gang sign or something?"

The boys all laughed and bent double, slapping thighs and backs.

RD draped one arm around Case's shoulders and pretended to laugh so hard that he needed help to remain standing. But after a long stretch of their theatrics, the boys finally quieted down and RD flashed the W in Case's face. "This is 'Whasup?' Not a gang sign, man. Coach would have us lapping-it until we puked ourselves inside out if he ever thought we was bangin'."

Case couldn't deny a sense of relief at that revelation. He flashed the sign back to RD. "Whasup?" He allowed a sheepish laugh to escape. "Glad to hear I won't have to off anyone in order to hang."

The boys all laughed again, if a bit less enthusiastically this time.

Case transitioned the conversation back to safer ground by

turning an appraising eye toward the house. "So the home place is sweet, man." He fist-bumped RD to show his appreciation.

RD shrugged. "My biological is never around, but he laid down for this place for my mom and me to live in."

"Your mom lets you have parties?" Case eased himself to a seat on the picnic table next to John.

"No, dawg! You think I have a death wish?" RD laughed. "She's away." He tilted a nod to the water. "On the main at a conference for her work."

Case set his beer down by his side and leaned back against his elbows that he propped against the table top. "Wish my pops would have to go to a conference." He grinned at the kid.

"Heard you want to go out for the soccer team, yeah?" RD changed the subject.

Case shrugged and released what he hoped sounded like a longsuffering sigh. "Can't. My pops said schoolwork has to come first."

"You always do what your daddy says?" That jab was from Hunter.

Case only shrugged and attempted to look like he felt he had no choice.

RD gave him a squint-eyed look. "Probably best anyhow. You don't look like you got the moves."

Case gave him a good-natured back-handed slap to the arm. "I got the moves any time you want to take me on. Why not here and now?" He swept a gesture to the grassy lawn. "You got a ball in that fancy house of yours?" He grinned at the kid to keep it lighthearted, but his pulse started thumping in earnest then. It had been quite some time since he'd been varsity captain of his team in high school. He'd only played a few pick-up games here and there over the years. He just hoped this kid wasn't some sort of soccer ninja or something.

He needed to keep up appearances if he was going to solidify this friendship.

RD hopped up and down and shook one hand like he'd been severely offended. But he grinned as he backed toward his house. "You are on like a light, sucka."

Case returned the grin. He didn't remove his elbows from the table but kept his forcibly relaxed pose while he motioned with his hands. "Bring it."

It only took a few minutes for Case to recognize that he could easily keep pace with RD. He was good, but Case had been too in his day. When Case was the first to score in the improvised goals made of a spectator on each side, RD groaned loudly but good-naturedly. He reached a hand out to Case and walked him through the motions of a multi-step handshake. "You alright, dawg."

After that the game evolved to include others standing around and they spent a good thirty minutes getting sweaty, and another thirty chasing the ball through the underbrush at the edge of the yard and one time even into the waves when a wayward kick sent it there. When they grew tired of soccer the party moved indoors.

Case kept an eye out, but he never saw anyone dispensing drugs, orange or otherwise. It was almost midnight when he decided that it was time for this party to break up. He fired off a quick text to Mick. *Go.*

Within minutes, the place was surrounded by cops and kids were sprinting away through the bushes. Those who didn't take off running were easily rounded up, and those who did run were only a few minutes behind them. Case was satisfied that he'd prevented anyone from driving home in their present conditions.

As planned, the officers cuffed Case and Ramon to the same post on the house's deck railing. One of the officers served RD with a search warrant for the premises and then they headed inside.

"Yo man, this is police brutality!" RD yanked dramatically at the handcuffs, clanking them against the post.

The officer only waved over his shoulder and continued into the house.

Case leaned close to Ramon, giving the house a worried scrutiny. "You don't have anything in there that you don't want them to find, do you?"

Ramon slumped down. "My mom's gonna off me!"

Case held his silence, unsure if Ramon meant that he did have something to hide, or if he was just talking about the party in general. After a long moment, he decided that pushing for a little information at this point couldn't hurt. He leaned closer. "You aren't the one selling the Fire, are you?"

RD spurted a laugh. "I ain't stupid, yo. I was just messin' with you when I asked if you could score me some. Trying to figure out if you was the dealer. Soccer is too important to me. Only thing in the house is the beer and stuff."

Case felt a wave of relief. He genuinely liked this kid and was really glad to hear that the worst that was going to happen to him was a few nights in jail until his mom got back to the island, and likely some community service for distributing alcohol to minors.

Another wash of horror swept over RD's face. "Coach is gonna off me too!" He moaned and yanked at the cuffs again, as though he might be able to reverse time with the action.

"Yeah, my dad too." Case could only hope that RD would learn an easy lesson from this situation.

A few minutes later when one of the officers stepped out of the house, Case gave him a subtle shake of his head. It didn't take long for them to be released from the handcuffs, Case into the care of his "extremely angry father" and RD into custody until his mother returned and could take charge of him.

As soon as they reached Mick's sedan, Case told Mick about the disappointing interruption of Chloe's mother.

Mick blew out a breath. "Yeah. She stormed the station, I guess, Chloe in tow. Demanded that Parker get down here and bust the party up immediately. Almost destroyed the whole op!"

Whatever had happened, it appeared they'd been able to stall long enough to keep to their plans, so Case pressed ahead. "Did you find anything in the house?"

Mick gave a frustrated shake of his head. "We'll know more once the chem analysis of the place comes back, but it looked clean. No signs of Fire that we could find."

When they reached the house, Case strolled over to their suspect board and turned RD's photo to face the wall. If the chem analysis came back clean, they would later put a red X to cross him off the list permanently. But for now, Case felt certain he was no longer a suspect.

He studied the profiles of the remaining suspects on the board. Principal Vaughan and his wife, Simon Hall, Ashley Adams, and Chloe Schumacher had all been at Harbor House the night Greg died and had opportunity to pass him the drugs. Kyra Radell, several of the parents, and the two police officers had all been crossed off the suspect list with red markers already. The two officers because they'd both voluntarily submitted to residue testing for both themselves and their vehicles, as well as a drug sniffing dog that had been brought over from the mainland. They had passed all the steps without a hitch. And both had an alibi of having been away at a Northwest Security and Police Conference Expo in Idaho when Mason Green, the most recent victim—well, before Greg—had died just a few weeks ago.

The video from Harbor House showed that the parents who'd been crossed off the list had never left the restaurant from the time Greg arrived till after he left, and none of them had come close enough to him to pass him a bag of drugs.

Several others who'd been in the restaurant had either walked close enough to Greg that they could have passed him something or moved to locations off the camera where it couldn't be proven what they'd done.

They were down to five suspects from the restaurant that night.

Case turned to face Mick. "Do we need to reconsider the possibility that Greg purchased the drugs elsewhere, kept his meeting with Simon, and then shot up afterwards in the parking lot?"

Mick rubbed one hand over his face. "No. I still feel that possibility is really slim. Greg's autopsy revealed that he'd been using the drug for quite some time. So he was probably itching for a hit the minute he got his hands on the product. I still say those people on the board are our best suspects."

Slowly, Case returned his scrutiny to the board. "I'm inclined to agree. Who do we go after next?"

Captain Danielson strode closer to the wall and tapped his forefinger against Chloe Schumacher's forehead. "I think this is our next step."

Case nodded even as a bit of dread clenched his stomach. Just when he'd put her on notice that he wasn't interested... "Right. I'll see what I can do. But for now"—he headed for his room with a wave over his shoulder—"I'm beat. And I have seven AM detention again in the morning. Night."

A grunt was the only reply he got, but it was more than he got most nights. Case brushed his teeth and then flopped into bed. But even though he was exhausted, with all the adrenaline still pumping through him and his thoughts going a hundred miles an hour to process and analyze all he'd seen tonight he wasn't going to be dropping off to sleep anytime soon. He put his mind to work trying to come up with a way to get information out of Chloe without making her think he was interested. Thoughts of being interested brought to mind a beautiful woman named Kyra Radell. And the next thing he knew, he was waking up early Saturday morning with her still on his mind.

His lips twisted into a sardonic smile as he sat up and scrubbed the sleep from his face. Maybe after detention this morning he could swing by her place and take her some coffee. She might have some ideas for how he should approach Chloe without making her think he hadn't meant the distance he'd put between them last night. Kyra could also call the station while he was there and, so help him, if Damian—who he'd phoned last night before heading to the party and told to expect the call—threw him under the bus, the man wasn't going to live to see another sunset.

Chapter 11

The Java and Juice coffee shop on this island wasn't half bad, but Case would have downed the brew even if it tasted like bilge water. Might as well face it. He was an addict. He tossed his empty coffee cup in the trash can outside of the school as he jogged up the stairs toward detention. Today it was to be held in the chemistry room if he wasn't mistaken.

When he opened the door to the chemistry room, surprise filled him. Principal Vaughan himself was the supervisor today.

Fortuitous.

He eased into his seat. Unless someone was late, only two other kids appeared to have merited discipline this week and he didn't recognize either of them. Leaning back in his chair he considered... Was Principal Vaughan the kind of teacher who would forbid the students from speaking a word? Or could he use this time to extract some information from the man?

There was only one way to find out, but how did he go about pressing subtly?

Maybe it was better to just approach the situation head-on. He picked up a pencil and bounced the eraser against his desk. "Too bad about Salazar. I mean, I only had him in one class and didn't know him that well, but he seemed pretty chill."

He watched the man's face, searching for any small tick or blanch that might reveal something, but he saw only sadness. Weariness.

Mr. Vaughan leaned back in his chair and ran both hands through his thinning hair. Removed his glasses and massaged the bridge of his nose. "Yes. It was a terrible tragedy. I hope none of you will feel the need to try out this new drug. It's obviously very dangerous. I pray the police will find the person responsible sooner rather than later."

The other two boys mumbled soft agreement.

So far, so good. Case pressed his luck. "Did you know him well?"

This time a muscle in Principal Vaughan's cheek did twitch, but again, Case read grief in the reaction and not guilt. "Since he was just a baby. His parents moved in next door to us almost sixteen years ago now. I can't imagine what they must be feeling. He was a good kid. Too good to go out like that. I only wish—well, I wish none of these deaths had happened." His expression morphed into full-on teacher mode. "You three listen. You're too good to do drugs. Don't ever let anyone make you feel like you need the high offered by a drug. It's temporary. It's destructive. And there are plenty of things in life that provide that high in a lasting way. Working hard to provide for your family. Building healthy relationships. Heck, even taking in a gorgeous sunset down at the beach with a pretty lady by your side." The two boys at the back of the room chuckled softly, but Case didn't miss the fact that the principal's voice had broken there at the end. The man paused to clear his throat.

The question remained... Was it out of guilt? Or a true concern for his students?

Case considered him carefully. He studied the man's eyes. It was easy to voice an emotion, but much harder to make the eyes match it. If truth needed to be discerned it was always important to pay attention to the eyes. Was this all an act? There was an actual glimmer of moisture in the man's lower lids. And a quaver in the hand that reached out for a Kleenex from the box on the corner of his desk. And a fathomless depth of grief reflected in the steady gaze the man pinned him with when he said, "I don't want one of you kids to be next, understand?"

No. Case didn't think that was an act. The man was truly broken with concern for his students, not guilt.

He nodded at the man and leaned back in his chair. "Yes, sir."

For now he would quit pestering the man with questions. Case didn't think he was their guy. When he got home that would be one less suspect on the high-priority list.

Detention had only been going for about ten minutes when the outer door of the classroom opened.

Case lifted his head from where he'd been half snoozing on his desk, and was instantly awake. What was Principal Vaughan's wife doing here?

The other night he'd thought her much younger than her husband, with maybe a little help from plastic surgery, but now he could see she was probably in her late forties. The too tight skin around her puffy lips and pencil-dark brows revealed she'd had more than *some* work done with the hopes of keeping herself looking younger. Way more than some.

Principal Vaughan's face lit up at the sight of her, though.

She returned his smile and sashayed toward him, one hand wrapped around the strap of the tan bag over her shoulder and the other holding out a metallic silver travel mug. "I swung by the house to get a few things. You forgot your coffee on the counter when you left."

Were they separated? That hadn't been in either file.

Case didn't miss the slight jolt her words gave the man. Had she purposely been trying to humiliate him? Or was he just sensitive to the separation? Had that been what he was so earnestly trying to convince her about at the restaurant the other night? To come back to him? Whatever it was, it only took the man a moment to recuperate.

"You're a life-saver." Mr. Vaughan accepted the cup and her quick kiss on the cheek.

And then to Case's further surprise, both of them turned their focus directly on him.

Mr. Vaughan stood and spoke to the other two detainees. "Boys, please stay in your desks. I'm just going to step out into the hall with Case and my wife for a moment." With that, the man pegged Case with a look and stretched his hand toward the door, indicating Case should precede them.

Case stood and moved out ahead of them, suppressing a nervous chuckle. Why was it that even though he was a fully grown adult working undercover, it never felt good to be singled out for discipline? And yet, this might be the perfect opportunity to find out more about the wife.

Could she be the drug dealer? He pictured her carefully painted full lips, flawless skin, and artificial nails, and huffed. Highly doubtful. A woman like her was likely more interested in redecorating her bedroom for the millionth time than manufacturing and distributing drugs.

Out in the hallway he paused, clasped his hands behind his back, and tried to look appropriately penitent. For what, he wasn't exactly certain. But you didn't get dragged out into the hallway by the principal and his wife unless you were in trouble.

Principal Vaughan tugged the chemistry room door closed, smiled, and lifted his hands, palms out. "I know you probably think you are in even more trouble. You aren't. But I do want you to spend some time talking with my wife."

Case's confusion grew. He tried to remember if he'd noticed what line of work the woman was in. The truth was they hadn't really paid that much attention to her. She was only on their list because she'd been at the restaurant and they hadn't gotten around to crossing her off yet. He turned his focus on her.

She smiled and stretched out a hand. "Hi Case. I'm Candice Vaughan. I'm a licensed psychologist, and work part-time for the school on an as-needed basis. I'm also the island's best real estate agent." She accompanied that with a quick wink of humor. "I understand you just moved here and this is already your second time in detention? I'd like to talk to you about that, if you are willing to speak with me?"

Case bounced a look between the two. A teen would probably say he didn't need the counseling, but the truth was, it would be good to spend some time with her. Confirm whether they'd been right to label her as low priority. Determine if they could cross her off their list. So instead of declining, he shrugged and folded his arms. "It's not like I have a choice, right?"

The Vaughan's exchanged a look and Mrs. Vaughan reached out and touched his shoulder to turn him toward the teachers' lounge just down the hall. "If you'll just give me a few minutes of your time, I'd really appreciate it. We care about you, and that's why I'm here." Her smile seemed genuine.

He let her lead the way, hearing the chemistry room door click shut behind them as Principal Vaughan returned inside.

"So... Moving right before your senior year must have been tough, huh?" Inside the teachers' lounge, Candice directed him toward a padded chair and moved to the small fridge in the corner, tugging it open. "There's Pepsi in here. You want one?"

More caffeine was always good but Case chose to only offer an indifferent shrug. "Sure."

She popped the tab as she brought it over, handing it to him before she smoothed her hands over her skirt and sank into the chair opposite him, setting her bag on the floor near her feet. "Tell me about your move? What brought you and your dad to our island?"

"My dad's work." Case took a sulky sip of the Pepsi. If she wanted a sullen teen boy, she would get one.

"And what does he do?"

"He's in insurance."

Mrs. Vaughan held her silence waiting for him to elaborate.

"The guy who used to cover the island moved to California or something. And my dad got transferred here." Case tried to look bored with the conversation.

"And does that bother you? That you have to pack up your life and move whenever your father gets transferred?"

Case was about to give her a reply when a phone chirped from the depths of her purse.

She offered an apologetic smile, but when she pulled it out to silence it he could have sworn that she turned three shades paler. "You know what?" She lifted the phone. "This is an emergency. I'm going to have to take this. Please forgive me."

She hustled him back to the chemistry room, poked her head through the door only long enough to tell her husband "Sorry, one of my other clients needs me right away," and then hurried off, heels clicking loudly on the tiles of the hallway.

Case sank into his chair to complete the last thirty minutes of detention in boredom. But things had just taken a turn. He only wished he knew what that turn was.

When he got home today he would turn Principal Vaughan's image to the wall.

But he would also move the man's wife, way up to the top of the priority list. Why had she turned so pale? Who was the phone call really from? Was it really a client of hers? And if so was it a real estate client? Or another client in need of her counseling services? Or maybe it was neither, but instead a partner in a drug manufacturing and selling business?

The odds were slim that a woman like her was the one they were after, but Case had been around this business long enough to know that you should never just dismiss people out of hand. Sometimes it was the ones who looked the most innocent who turned out to be guilty.

They were down to four priority suspects. Ashley Adams and Simon Hall were still maybes in his book.

Chloe remained his number one suspect. She at the very least knew some things they needed to know. He planned to try and connect with her today.

But Mrs. Vaughan had just put herself in the position of close second with her strange behavior.

Case reminded himself there were a couple suspects still only marginally crossed off the list. He sighed. Why did it feel like they were no closer to an arrest than they had been at the beginning of this op?

Chapter 12

The text came through at seven thirty.

Kyra rolled over with a groan and hugged her pillow tighter as she snuggled deeper into the warmth of her blankets.

Saturday! she mentally complained.

But only moments later, her phone chimed again. Kyra pried open one eye and fumbled for the phone on her night stand.

She frowned. The new texts were from the name "Anonimus." The first one read, **I know who is selling Fire.** Followed by, **But I'm scared to tell.**

Suddenly wide awake, Kyra flopped back on her pillow and stared at the ceiling. Her first thought was of Case who just last night had asked her not to meddle in this investigation. Her second thought was to remind herself that she still wasn't one hundred percent sure he even *was* a cop.

"Gah!" She sat up abruptly and dropped the phone back onto the charger. She needed a shower and a cup of coffee before deciding how to proceed.

From her dresser, she grabbed a pair of jeans and an old blue Levi's T-shirt that promised comfort, then headed for the bathroom.

She took longer in the shower than usual because her mind was spinning through considerations of what to do about the new texts. She should go directly to the police with them. But if Case was a cop and truly here to investigate the drugs, then he was the logical one to report the incident too. Yet how could she do that until she knew without a shadow of doubt that he really was a cop? And there were plenty of doubts. All night long she'd tossed and turned. One moment thinking she should just trust him, and the next thinking there was no possible way he could actually be an undercover cop and telling herself not to get duped. She finally gave up on the problem and shut off the water that had turned tepid before it could swing all the way to cold.

Her hair was still wet and wrapped in a towel when a knock sounded on her kitchen door. Her heart started pounding even before she rounded the corner and saw that it was indeed Case, face concealed once more with the large hood of a sweatshirt. She felt the familiar swirl of confusion that seemed to grip her whenever he was around. What was it about him that stirred her with nothing more than his presence?

One look into those ice green eyes and she was practically ready to throw the door wide open and tell him she believed every word he'd said. Confide in him about the texts she'd just received.

She must have given him too long of a questioning look through the glass, because after a moment he hefted the brown paper sack he held, as though that was reason enough for her to let him in.

Even as she unlatched the chain, she bemoaned the realization that she didn't have even a swipe of makeup on yet. And then her irritation with herself doubled and doubled again. Lives were on the line and she was concerned about her appearance?

Reminding herself to proceed with all caution, she pulled open the door but didn't move back to let him in.

He offered her that charming smile that was becoming so familiar. "Morning."

She remained where she stood, folding her arms, because she needed the shield that put between them. "Morning." She waited for him to state his purpose.

He didn't seem to be in a hurry. His gaze started at the towel around her hair, slipped the length of her, and then meandered its way back to the towel.

How could the man make her feel caressed without ever touching her? Goose flesh pebbled her arms. She clenched her fists. *Even if he is a cop, a relationship in this situation can go nowhere.*

"Aren't you concerned one of my neighbors might see you?" She asked the question even though she had no neighbor to the back and the likelihood of one of the other two being able to see who he was through the wisteria that grew thick along the arbor of the back porch was slim. She planned to throw every test she could at the man until she was one hundred percent certain one way or the other of his identity, cop or student.

Cradling the bag of groceries against one hip, he leaned a shoulder into the doorframe, which put him closer than she liked, but if she backed away it would be like giving ground.

He tipped a nod to the east. "Those neighbors left on vacation yesterday, so no one is home." With a nod in the other direction, he said, "And Mrs. Hix left to take Saunders for his morning walk about five minutes ago. So, unless you plan on keeping me out here for another twenty minutes, I should be good." His mouth tipped in humor. "Besides, I knew you'd want to call the Everett PD right away this morning to put your lingering doubts to rest. I might have been here sooner, but I had detention this morning." His eyes sparkled with the bad-boy appeal that had likely gotten him assigned to detention in the first place as his gaze swept over her once more. "But it looks like if I'd have arrived any earlier, you might have still been in the shower. Anyhow, the station doesn't open till eight on Saturdays."

Kyra was still uncertain. Still pondering what to do about the texts. "What's in the bag?"

"Kona coffee and stuff to make Swedish pancakes and blintz for breakfast."

He was so close she could feel the warmth of him invading her space. She swallowed. "That sounds good." She said the words that indicated she should invite him inside, yet somehow her feet remained stuck fast.

Those full lips tilted up at the corners again. He spoke so softly she might not have heard him if her every attention hadn't been focused on him in that moment. "If I'm going to cook, you have to let me in. But if I'm not going to cook"—his gaze lowered to her mouth—"I can think of some other ways to pass the time."

Her feet suddenly loosened from the floorboards and she stepped back, sweeping a hand for him to enter. Was her face as red as it felt? She spun away from him. It was probably a huge mistake to let him in. But what was done, was done. "You cook. I'm going to go dry my hair." And put on makeup, but she left that part out.

"But making breakfast suddenly holds so little appeal," he teased.

She suppressed a smile and kept walking. Bad boy charm, indeed.

"Don't rush on my account!" he called after her as she hurried from the room.

By the time she felt presentable, the wonderful rich scent of the Kona tantalized her. She grabbed her cell phone from the charger by her bed and headed back to the kitchen. It was now almost eight thirty. The police station should be open.

Case was just pouring coffee into two mugs when she

pushed through the door. Two plates held some sort of thin pancakes rolled into round tubes and filled with something creamy. Strawberries were sliced across the top of each roll. She tried to remember what he'd called it.

He paused mid-pour and gave her a look that could only be interpreted as appreciative. She felt her cheeks warm again and pointedly drew his attention back to the food. "This looks good. What did you call it?"

He returned the coffee carafe to its spot and clutched at his chest dramatically. "You've never heard of blintz?!"

She wrinkled her nose. "Should I have?"

"Oh man. Now I'm worried we might not be able to be friends." He tossed her a rapid-fire wink.

She rolled her eyes at him.

He grinned. "Sit." He swept a gesture to the table, then followed her and set one of the plates before her with a flourish and a little bow.

She couldn't help the chuckle that escaped. "You really are enjoying this, aren't you?"

"I always enjoy spending time with a beautiful woman." He set his own plate and cup across from her and sat down.

Her brows arched. "Sounds like you make it a regular occurrence."

He snorted. "I guess I dug my own hole on that one." His face lost all humor. "In all seriousness, I do find you attractive. But as you can imagine this really isn't a good time for... anything new in my life. I really came by today to ask you for some advice. And to see the look on your face when you finally realize that I'm not just a kid trying to pull one over on you." The glint returned to his eyes.

She smirked. "We can take care of that right now." Absentmindedly, she took a bite of one of the pancakes as she reached for her phone, but froze the moment the smooth cheesy filling and tart sweetness of the strawberries danced across her tongue. "Oh man! This is so good!"

Case curled his hands around his coffee mug and smiled at her over the rim, elbows on the table. "Told you."

"What's in this?"

He shook his head. "Nope. No getting distracted. Call the police department first."

She acquiesced, but not before taking another bite and rolling her eyes in delight. She covered her mouth with one hand and spoke around the mouthful. "Who am I supposed to ask for again?"

"Detective Damian Packard. Put it on speaker. I promise I won't say a word." He stuffed his mouth full of pancakes as if to prove it.

"He's really going to be at work on a Saturday morning?"

Case's answer was to nudge her hand holding the phone and give a short nod.

Kyra dialed the number she'd looked up the evening before and set the phone on the table between them. Only a moment later a woman answered. "Everett Police Department, is this an emergency?"

"Uh, no. I'd like to speak to Detective Damian Packard please?"

"Do you have a case number?"

Kyra felt her pulse give a happy skitter. The man at least existed. "Uh no. I'm…working with…"

"His partner," Case mouthed.

"His partner."

There was a moment of pause on the other end of the line. Then, "Alright. Let me put you through. Just a moment."

The phone rang twice.

"This is Detective Packard. How can I help you?" The man

had a nice voice—deep, mellow, and smooth, with just a touch of an accent that she couldn't quite peg.

Kyra's mouth was suddenly dry. She should have thought through how to word her question. "Ah yes, detective. My name is Kyra Radell. I'm a teacher out on North Sound Island. How are you this morning?"

"Good. What can I do for you?" There was definite hint of humor in his tone, but also an indication that he was a busy man and she should get on with it.

"Well, I'm calling to ask if you know an officer named Case Lexington?"

A long pause ensued from the other end of the line. "Lexington? No. Can't say as I know anyone by that—"

"Pack! I swear you are about to find yourself on my bad side!" Case growled from his position across the table.

Over the line Detective Packard started laughing. "Oh, so you are there. You can't blame me for a little retribution! Wasn't it just a few weeks ago you tried to convince Carina that I'd transferred to Miami Beach?"

Case's eyes narrowed, but his lips quirked with humor.

Kyra was outright laughing now, her relief at having Case known by the department making her almost giddy. "So you are willing to vouch that Case is indeed an officer?"

Damian's chair squeaked as though he'd just leaned back in it. "Blond hair? Green eyes? Sourpuss frown on his face right about now? Yeah, that's him."

Kyra grinned at Case. "Alright, we'll let you go. Thank you."

The chair squeaked again and this time Kyra heard the distinct thud of feet hitting the floor. "Yeah. No worries. Take care Case, you hear? What's the count, man?"

Case reached for the phone. "Always on two, Pack. Always on two."

"For sure." Damian's dismissal was casual, but she could hear true respect and care for each other in the men's voices.

Case punched the off circle and then slid her phone back toward her.

"What does the count always being on two mean?"

Case shrugged. "When you give a perp the countdown, you tell them three or five, or whatever number. But you always act on two. It's sort of his way of telling me to be careful. Anyhow," he leaned into the slats of his chair and folded his arms. "Believe me now?"

Kyra swallowed, suddenly feeling a wash of huge responsibility for keeping this man of the law safe. "Yes. I do. So your father is…?"

Case chuckled. "He's actually my boss."

Kyra felt the burden she'd been carrying all morning lift a little. Now she could tell him about the texts without worry. She opened her mouth and started to speak, but he beat her to it.

"Good. Now let me get to the reason I came." There was a subtle shift in Case's tone, a little more of a take charge note and a little less the ne'er-do-well senior who'd slept through several of her classes. "I need some advice about Chloe."

Kyra almost choked on the bite of blintz in her mouth. That was the last thing in the world she'd expected him to say.

He raised his hands. "I know. I'm obviously not interested in her and I made that very clear to her last night, but now she's jumped to the top of our suspect list and the likelihood of me getting all the information I need from her in one pass is slim to none. So I'm going to need to spend some time with her without leading her on. Got any ideas on that?"

"You need a girlfriend."

He blinked at her.

Her face blazed. "I mean, not in real life, but maybe you

could invent one. That should allow you to be friends with her but still keep it platonic."

"I already told her I have a girl back home."

Disappointment slipped through her. So he was already taken. Of course a guy like him would already have a woman in his life. She forced a casual nod. "That should be good then."

Case shook his head. "She made it pretty clear she wasn't going to let that stop her."

Girls these days. Kyra couldn't believe that a wash of jealousy had just swept through her over a teenage girl with a crush. Or maybe it had more to do with whoever the woman on the other side of the water was. Had that relationship developed after he'd flirted so outrageously with her in the salon that day? Or was he just as much of a womanizer as his earlier comment about enjoying spending time with beautiful women seemed to imply?

Realizing he was still waiting for her response, she hurried to say, "Uh, well... I could try to find out something from her if you need me to?"

Case practically leapt to his feet. "No." He paced to the kitchen island and leaned into his palms.

Kyra was taken aback by the abrupt response.

He looked over at her. "I'm sorry. It's just... I don't want you involved with this investigation. It's dangerous. Whether you believe me or not."

She leveled him with a look. "I'm already involved simply because I work at the school. I can't just ignore these kids. They need someone they can confide in."

He spun toward her. "So you haven't changed your mind about what you said in class on Friday?"

She shrugged. Now it was confession time. "It's sort of too late to change my mind."

He stiffened. Studied her leerily. "What do you mean?"

With a sigh, she rose and walked closer to him. "I haven't told you this yet, but when I was just a freshman in high school, my older brother got into drugs. It was like overnight he became a different person."

Case reached out to squeeze her shoulder. "I'm so sorry."

Kyra pressed ahead, keeping the details as sparse as possible. "He took his own life within a year. I chose then to become a teacher with the hope that I could maybe help other kids who might find themselves in that same place. When you told me you were a cop, I didn't know whether to believe you but I still wanted to help. So I told all my classes about the option to contact me anonymously. And now there's this..." Placing her phone on the counter between them, she pressed the icon to pull up her texting ap, then brought up this morning's messages.

Case picked up her phone and read the texts. His shoulders drooped as though the weight of the world had just been dumped on them. "Well, I guess you are involved now whether I like it or not." He lifted his gaze to hers. "Promise me you'll be careful, and that you'll run everything by me before you make any decisions?"

Kyra was just fine with that. She'd already been uncertain of even how to respond to this morning's messages. "I promise."

"I especially want you to be careful around Simon Hall. Don't go out to dinner alone with him, or anything like that."

Kyra dipped her chin and narrowed her eyes at him. "Simon? Really? Because from my interactions with him he seems to genuinely care about the kids. He was pretty broken up about Greg Salazar's death."

Case shrugged noncommittally. "There's just something about the guy I don't like. He's right up there at the top of my list along with Chloe, and another person who just came to my attention this morning. And maybe Ashley. Anyhow"—he lifted her phone—"you didn't respond yet?"

She shook her head. Wrapped her arms around herself to ward off a sudden chill. "I wanted to show it to you, but only once I was certain you were really a cop."

"Mind if I reply?"

She shook her head. "Please, feel free."

He tapped in a few words and hit send before setting it down on the counter.

"What did you say?"

His thumbs tapped out a rhythm on the counter as he stared at the phone as though impatient for a quick response. "I asked them if they were safe right now."

Horror raced down Kyra's spine. "I should have thought of that! Why didn't I ask that right away! What if something's happened and I didn't even respond!"

Case covered her hand—a gesture that both told her to calm down and offered comfort. "I'm sure they're fine. It's highly unlikely they took time to text you if they were in danger. It's just always good to be sure." His tone held encouragement.

Kyra withdrew her hand from the too tempting warmth and appeal of his touch.

They both stared at the phone. Kyra realized she was almost holding her breath and released it. She frowned and forked her fingers into her hair, needing to break the silence. "Will you be able to figure out who it is by their number?"

He shook his head. "Probably not. There are all kinds of ways people can send anonymous texts these days, but we'll certainly give it a try."

"Anonymous texts?" She hadn't even known that was a thing.

The phone chimed and Case snatched it up.

Kyra crowded close to read over his shoulder. **_Yes. I'm fine. I don't think s he would hurt me._**

She? Or was the 'S' a typo and it was meant to read 'he'?

Kyra glanced over as Case's brows raised, and only in that moment did she realize they were so close they were standing shoulder to shoulder. She eased away. "If it is a she, I guess that blows your theory about Simon Hall."

"Maybe." Case admitted before he smirked. "Unless this is Simon Hall trying to throw you off the scent. Or unless that 'S' isn't supposed to be there at all."

Kyra folded her arms, feeling defensive. "You're just jealous." Her face blazed. She couldn't believe she'd just blurted that out even if she partially thought it was true.

Case's gaze swept over her and then a glint of humor touched his eyes. "I guess that might be true. Do I have anything to be jealous about?"

Was sweat actually breaking out on her forehead? She paced over to the window to put some space between them and tugged the curtain to one side to peer out. "I told you the other day that I'm not looking for another relationship right now, and I meant it. Plus, I'd never date a colleague."

"What about a student?"

She spun toward him, ready to let him have it, but stopped at the twist of mischief on his lips. She flapped her hand toward the phone. "Can we just get back to the present situation, please?"

Case chuckled, but his expression turned serious when he returned his focus to the phone. He studied the screen for a moment before asking. "Both texts came through about seven thirty?"

She nodded. "One right after the other."

"Interesting." He tapped one knuckle against his lips, staring toward the ceiling and seemingly considering some possibilities before he finally stopped pacing and returned his focus to the text message. "In situations like this it's generally best to give them lots of room and not make them feel pressured. I could ask if it's a he or a she to try to fish for a little more information, but that might spook them." He spoke his message as he typed. "Well, if you change your mind, I'm happy to listen." He tapped a few more keys, informing her that he was forwarding the message to his boss so they could check out the number, then he handed the phone back to Kyra. "I'm betting you won't hear back for a while, but if they respond again, please let me know right away." He glanced at his watch. "For now, I really have to get going. I'm supposed to meet Chloe at the beach in half an hour. No other thoughts for me on that front?"

Kyra stuffed her phone into her back pocket. "Well, you could always bring your girlfriend from back home over here and let her see you two together. That might make the reality of your unavailability more real to her, but still allow you to maintain a friendship where you can get some information."

Case rubbed the back of his neck. "The only problem with that is she doesn't exist."

Kyra's heartrate gave a little spike. "She doesn't?"

But Case was still talking, not seeming to have heard her. "Too bad, too, because that's actually not a bad idea. I think Chloe might open up more if I did have a girlfriend. She's the type who might do a little bragging to try to impress me if there was a little competition."

Kyra felt her eyes widen, because she suddenly had a really crazy idea.

Back when she was taking her theater arts major in college she'd routinely made herself over into someone else. She'd often taken pleasure in tricking her friends into thinking she was someone entirely different. They'd always been shocked when she revealed herself to them. If Case needed a girlfriend, *she* could play the part.

She opened her mouth to tell him so, but then snapped it shut again. He would only tell her once again that it was too dangerous and he didn't want her involved. Better to act and then ask for forgiveness later. But she ought to feel out the situation a little more first. "You could always have someone else pose as your girl?"

He shook his head. "Can't. That would involve bringing more people into the loop. And there isn't time at this point to get another officer over here from the mainland. At least not for my meeting with her this morning. But don't worry about it." He was already heading for the kitchen door. "I'll figure it out. Be safe and let me know if you get any more texts."

Kyra's heart raced. She needed more information if she was going to pull this off. And it had to happen today because she'd promised Lainey that she would come over to the mainland and go to church with her family tomorrow since the twins were being dedicated. "Where did you say you were going to meet her?"

Case paused and eyed her questioningly. But after a moment he must have decided that it couldn't hurt to tell her. "At the park down near the ferry landing."

Perfect. "Okay. Bye." She lifted a hand. "I'll stay in touch. See you soon."

Sooner than he realized.

"Right." He nodded. "See you Monday, if not before."

They repeated the routine with her taking out the trash, which felt less tense in the daylight, and then he leapt her fence and disappeared from sight.

Kyra turned for her room with a huge grin on her face. She couldn't wait to surprise him. A quick check of the ferry schedule revealed that she had just enough time to pull off her transformation.

Chapter 13

Anger burned cold, like a cauldron of frothy liquid nitrogen lodged just below breastbone and heart.

I knew Kyra Radell was trouble the minute I laid eyes on her. Offering kids an anonymous way to tattle. *Gah!* But little did they all know they were beaten before they'd even begun. "I'm smarter than all of you put together." The words rasped past lips that had hardly spoken a word since yesterday.

Thumbs tapped out a rhythm on the steering wheel. Parked just across and down the street from Kyra's house, the time had come to decide and take action. It was imprudent to simply sit by while students smiled in your face and then betrayed you the moment your back was turned. If that little minx, Chloe Schumacher, had betrayal on her mind, it was time to plug up the potential leak. At least it was clear she was still fearful enough that she was having second thoughts. What would have happened if she'd revealed all?

Nausea roiled.

Indigestion burned an already tight throat.

The little traitor!

Popping the lid off the bottle of Tums on the passenger seat was easy. Downing three of the chalky tablets, not so much. Lips twisted in disgust. Nasty stuff. Always leaving such a gritty paste on the tongue. A swig of cold coffee from the travel mug only made the taste worse.

Slamming the mug back into the holder eased some of the irritation. But not enough.

What to do? What to do? *Think!*

No one had come or gone from Kyra's house yet this morning and she hadn't made any calls, so maybe she hadn't decided what to do about the texts yet. But the cloned ap clearly showed that she'd read the betraying texts from Chloe.

Wait!

Even as panic nipped at an already thready pulse, letters started appearing in the ap. She was replying right now!

A huff of ironic disgust escaped at the first reply.

She wanted to know if the kid was safe? She might be for now, but not for long. Traitors didn't deserve to keep breathing. That much had been made more than clear to every kid who'd ever been invited to partake of Fire. It wouldn't be hard to find her and take care of her. It needed to be done today before she got up the courage to reveal more than she already had.

Thankfully, the text had arrived on Kyra's phone after this morning's surveillance session had already begun. It would have been crazy-making not to know if she'd rushed right out of her house to head to the police station with those texts. Even now it was a little surprising that she hadn't called someone or even texted someone for advice on what to do.

It was Saturday, maybe she'd been sleeping in a little?

A curl of uncertainty wormed through the nausea. Was Kyra being too laid back about the texts? Could someone be in the house with her? Giving her advice? She seemed like the type who would immediately seek out advice on what to do in a situation like this.

Don't be paranoid.

The texted reply came back.

Yes. I'm fine. I don't think s he would hurt me.

A drop of sweat dripped onto the phone despite the fact

that it was a balmy sixty-nine degrees outside. *Calm down. She didn't reveal anything too important with that.* The mistake in the type was bound to leave just as many questions as it answered. Still, it was time to go find the kid and silence her before she revealed anything more.

It would kill two birds with one stone. Stop the leak. And send a message to the rest of the clientele that silence equaled life.

The curtain at Kyra's kitchen window moved slightly.

Just enough to send heartrate skyrocketing. Scrunched down behind the steering, wheel it was hard to see past the glare on her window glass.

Had she noticed the car parked down the street? The curtain dropped back into place. But she didn't rush out to her porch to get a better look.

After a moment, tension eased a little. That wasn't saying much considering how terrifying this morning had been.

Maybe laying off production of Fire for a bit was called for?

No!

This was not going to be a setback. All the supplies for the ramped-up production had just arrived this week. The final shipment, signed for yesterday after school, held the last ingredient needed. This next batch was going to be the biggest, and most lucrative, yet.

Nervous fingers fiddled with the nob of the gearshift. Squeezed it so hard that a tremor worked all the way to scrunched toes.

Relax!

Purposefully, muscles eased their stricture. One long slow breath in. One long slow breath out. Another pair of Tums crunched down.

All would be fine again before lunchtime. Chloe would never be able to undertake betrayal again.

But it remained to be seen if Kyra Radell could be allowed to live. If students were going to keep taking her up on her offer, she was going to have to go. What if one of them really did leave a note in her assignment inbox? And it couldn't be retrieved before Kyra found it? That was a method of communication that couldn't be hacked.

A sigh slipped free, even as the engine turned over.

Yes, Kyra Radell just might have to be dealt with. But for now, there were other matters to attend to. The sports car's engine purred quietly as Kyra's house slid by on the left.

Tonight, there should be plenty of time for more surveillance of her. And if things went as planned, there would no longer be a leak to worry about.

Kyra's transformation was complete. She sat back and looked at herself in the mirror. She grinned. It always amazed her what a lot of makeup and a little bit of ingenuity could do to change someone's appearance.

She'd added a prosthetic to widen her forehead just slightly—one that she'd previously used for a show where she'd played the part of an older lady, but it had worked just as well here to transform her to a slightly younger woman. A darker foundation than she normally wore gave her a bit more of a tan than she usually had. She'd also applied tanning lotion to both her arms and her legs. Colored contacts changed her eye color from blue to green, and fake lashes combined with the heavier than usual makeup, worked together to make her eyes look a little more slanted and exotic. Bright red lips, a stick-on beauty mark, and a dark wig swept into a curly updo finished the facial transformation.

For her outfit, a black leather miniskirt paired with a black tank-top, knee-height black stiletto boots, and a gothic spiked leather necklace-collar changed her from everyday-schoolteacher to gothic-biker-chick.

Now all that was left was to surprise Case at the park and prod Chloe into revealing whatever it was she might know. Unless the student who'd texted her decided to reveal more information, this was their best shot.

Hopefully, Chloe would be appropriately jealous and try to get his attention by spilling whatever information Case thought she might be hiding.

She stuffed her phone into the top of one of the boots, more because she didn't like to be without it than because she felt like she was going to need it. Then, popping a piece of gum into her mouth, Kyra headed for the door.

Her hand was already on the knob when she froze. "You're such a goofball!"

She couldn't just waltz out her front door dressed like this. First of all, any of her neighbors who saw her would think she was off her rocker, and secondly, word spread much too fast in small communities like this.

She needed to go out the back. She could take the trail through the woods at the back of her property and come out just on the edge of the park right near the ferry landing, which was perfect for her pretense that she'd only arrived on the ferry this morning. The only problem would be if she saw anyone on the trail along the way. But she'd jogged that trail every day since moving here and hadn't once run into anyone walking along it. It was too bad really. People on this island lived in a virtual paradise, but it was all so normal and ho-hum to most of them. She would just have to take the chance that no one would be out there, or at least wouldn't recognize her if they were.

She paused before opening the gate in her back fence that led right onto the community's walking trail. She listened for a moment, but heard no footsteps crunching in the gravel that lined the path. With a breath for courage, and a quick prayer for protection for all involved, she hurried through the gate and shut it behind her. A glance up and down the trail relieved some of her tension. No one in sight.

She started off in the direction of the ferry landing, immediately realizing that stiletto walking boots probably hadn't been the best choice for this rather rugged path. But there was nothing for it but to push ahead now. She would be to the park inside of ten minutes.

That was when she heard someone jogging her way—just beyond the bend in the trail and coming toward her from the direction of the park.

If she kept going they were going to pass right by each other! Why today of all days did someone have to be out here?

Frantic glances offered nothing substantial enough to hide her. To her right were a few small trees interspersed between the path and the other back fences of the rest of her neighborhood. But the trunks were too small to conceal her. And to her left, the hillside rose quite steeply. There were larger trees and some bushes about eight feet up, but her heels would never make it up that incline—not to mention the thick carpet of pine needles that would turn over under her feet the moment she tried to climb the hill. Besides, there was no time. It would look even more suspicious if she were caught trying to scramble out of sight.

Her heart hammered. Her only option was to keep walking and pretend like it was totally normal for a woman to be trekking along a gravel path wearing four-inch heels. She pressed forward, wishing she had thought to bring her small purse and pepper spray. She didn't usually travel anywhere without it, but today her mind had been on other things—like the reaction she was going to get from Case when she surprised him.

The jogger came around the corner, and she almost lost her footing altogether.

It was Simon Hall! He was wearing a green Seattle Sounders shirt. Was sweaty. And panting. He gave her the merest nod of a glance, lifted one finger in greeting, and moved right on past her.

Kyra released a breath she didn't know she'd been holding. And then a thrill of excitement zipped through her. He hadn't recognized her! There hadn't even been a hitch in his step!

She scanned him over her shoulder. Odd that he wore a backpack while jogging, right? But then, the man had been a little odd from the first moment he'd introduced himself to her on the first day of school.

Anyhow... None of that mattered! Her disguise was working!

Now her next feat would be if she could blend in with the crowd coming off the ferry. For her plan to work it had to look to Chloe like she'd just come across the water.

It actually took her less than her predicted ten minutes to get to the park, so she arrived a little before the ferry, but a peek through the gate that led into the park showed the ship just gliding into the landing. She shut the gate, forcing herself to wait a few more moments before going into the park.

If today was true to form, in just a few minutes a crowd would sweep past her heading toward all the tourist shops in town. She would just open the gate and meld in with them. Then she'd have to find Case, but that shouldn't be too hard. The park wasn't that large.

Time seemed to stretch interminably. Come on! How long did it take to dock a ferry and allow the passengers to disembark?

She tossed a glance over her shoulder. What would she do if Simon Hall came back? It would surely look suspicious for her to be lingering here. Had he left his car at the park? Would he be coming back this way? And if he did see her? Would word get out that she hadn't really come across on the ferry after all? Was she about to blow Case's cover?

She pressed one hand to her chest. Maybe she should rethink this...

But her fears were unjustified because just then she heard the first snippets of excited conversation from a group of tourists leaving the boat.

She'd done it! She eased open the gate and merged onto the cement walkway just behind the leading gaggle of ladies, giving herself a little fist pump of encouragement.

This undercover stuff might not be so hard after all.

Now to find Case.

Chapter 14

Case drove to Landing Park, pulled into a space, and took a moment to assess. He ran through the questions he and Captain Danielson had discussed the evening before.

How was Chloe involved in all this? Was she at the top of the distribution chain? The only one in the chain? Merely one of the middle men? Or did she know absolutely nothing at all and he'd been wrong in his suspicions this whole time?

Hopefully he'd have some answers by the end of the day. He took a breath, tossed up a prayer for favor and protection, and then eased himself from his car.

Chloe wasn't hard to spot. She was pacing near the tall craggy fountain at the center of the park. It was composed of a towering stack of rock slabs that cascaded water into a clear pool below. Rugged river rock, about two and a half feet high, walled in the pool. Topped with flat stones, the wall offered a place to sit along the perimeter of the water feature.

Was Chloe alone? She kept looking around and had jumped twice. She looked more nervous than a lap dog on the Fourth of July. He scanned the park. It never hurt to be too careful even though he doubted there was any danger here today.

On this sunny Saturday on perhaps one of the last warm days before winter set in, the place was jam-packed. He passed a family seated on a red and white quilt, eating a picnic lunch, and across the way a father played a rousing round of frisbee with his three kids. Several women with exercise mats appeared to be doing yoga on the east side of the park. And even Principal Vaughan apparently hadn't been able to resist the temptation of today's sun. He was sitting on a bench, drinking coffee, and chatting off and on with frisbee-dad. And to the southwest, the Salish Sea, part of the Puget Sound, stretched out with a snow-topped Mount Baker capping the scene in the distance.

Too bad he was here to work because he could really let himself relax in this environment, otherwise. Maybe he'd have to look for a house out here at some point.

He was turning back toward Chloe when one of the yoga women bent into a stretch and the woman behind her caught his attention. Ashley Adams.

He made a mental note to check and see if she did yoga here on a regular basis or if this was an anomaly in her routine. For now, she appeared innocent and harmless enough.

The ferry whistle blew, drawing his attention to the vessel which had just docked at the pier. Workers on the bow called directions to one another as they tossed three-inch thick tie-lines around the cleats on the dock and cinched the boat to the shore.

Chloe spotted him and raised an arm in greeting as a passel of tourists spilled off the ferry, chattering and excited about their excursion to the island.

He paused to let them pass in front of him.

A leggy brunette in a black leather mini skirt separated herself from the crowd and called his name—loudly. She waved one arm and grinned, giving a little bounce of excitement, hurrying toward him.

He searched his memory as he took in the woman's features. Slender. Curvaceous. Beautiful. But not someone he knew.

He frowned. He must have been mistaken. She must have

said someone else's name. He glanced back to see who she might be so excited to see, but no one was there.

She bounced over to him, calling as she came, "Case! You came to get me? How did you even know I was going to be here? You silly! It was supposed to be a secret!" Before he could even think what to say, she threw her arms around him.

What the—? On reflex his hands came up to cup her waist. His mind was still scrambling to put a name to the admittedly-exquisite body in his arms. He came up blank. His heart thundered. Was he about to be outed as a cop? Where did he know this woman from? And why did she think he was here to meet her?

He was about to push her away to ask how she knew him when she whispered in his ear, "It's Kyra."

A wave of shock froze him in place. No way. He never would have recognized her! Not even her voice sounded the same, but what—

She pulled back just enough to curve her hands around his face and continued to whisper. "What do you say we make Chloe jealous? Then you dump me and go off with her and hopefully she spills everything she knows to you?"

He studied her. Really studied her. But he couldn't see anything of Kyra in the woman before him. Not even her eyes were the right color.

Caution surged. Was this some sort of trap? He took a step back. "I don't know what—"

She curled her fingers into the hair at the nape of his neck, refusing to let him go. "You just left my house not long ago." Now *that* voice was Kyra's. "I showed you texts on my phone. I teach you English and PE but we met at my sister's nail salon where I told you about Roscoe and turned you down for a date." All this was spoken low and intimately, as though she might be whispering sweet-nothings to him.

Only Kyra could know all that stuff, even if someone could make their voice sound like her. "But how—"

She smiled softly. "I majored in drama in college. Now look happy to see me or Chloe is going to know something is wrong." Her voice was back to that of the charming goth girl.

Look happy to see her? Alright.

He kissed her.

Felt her gasp. But that served her right for taking him unaware like that. It was only a moment before her surprise melded into a passionate response.

The softness of her lips registered and sent a surge of endorphins to every extremity. His hands slipped to the curve of her lower back, tugging her closer, but he kept the kiss slow and tame, despite the fact that everything in him urged for more.

She gave as good as she got, wrapping her arms around his neck, and working her lips firmly across his.

A little sigh of pleasure eased from her, heightening his desire to take the kiss a little further. He slid one hand to the back of her neck, intending to pull her closer, but the feel of the dog collar choker jolted him back to the present. This was only work, no matter that he would love for it to be so much more. He pulled back from her and settled her head against his shoulder. His eyes fell closed and he swallowed as he fought to regain his clarity.

Innocent Kyra, with all her hopes and ambitions for the good of her students was here in his arms. And all he could think about now was that if something went wrong today he might not be able to keep her safe. He perused the people gathered in the park. Nothing seemed out of the ordinary, but he kept his focus vigilant as he lowered his mouth to whisper in her ear, "You shouldn't be here!"

She lifted her gaze to his and laid a finger across his lips.

"You said yourself that this was a good idea that might help you get information."

She had him there.

He swallowed. Skimmed the crowd again. He liked the caress of her finger across his lips just a little too much.

She tilted her head and moved her hand to play with his hair. "Did you tell her a name? She's shooting daggers at me with her eyes." She winked.

He racked his brain as he glanced over his shoulder.

All the tourists had passed now and Chloe was eyeing them with a decided gleam of jealousy in her expression.

Had he told Chloe a name? No. The number one rule undercover was when you had to lie, make it vague. You could always add in more details if the need arose. And it looked like the need had just arisen.

Lacing his fingers with Kyra's, he turned to face the angry teen, tugging Kyra after him. "Chloe, I'd like you to meet my girlfriend, Darcy."

"Hi." Kyra draped herself against his arm in a perfect mimicry of how a teen couple might behave, but still managed to stretch her hand out to Chloe. The gesture was friendly, but at the same time said, "Back off. He's mine."

Case bit back a grin. He had to admit, she was good. But her presence here continued to have him on high alert. Another glance around the park, however, revealed nothing out of the ordinary. Some of his anxiety eased. It wasn't like she'd tagged along on an undercover gun-buy. This was just him getting some information from a teen.

Hopefully.

He returned his focus to Chloe. Now to see if he could propel this situation along.

"So Chloe, listen..." He drew Kyra in front of him, wrapped her in his arms and dropped his chin against her shoulder.

Forcing himself to ignore how much he liked the feel of her curled against him, he pressed ahead. "Darcy and I would like to have a good time this weekend, if you catch my meaning."

With a silly teenage giggle, Kyra relaxed her head back against his shoulder and wrapped her arms over his. "Case does know how to show a girl a good time, but I'm sure you wouldn't know." The words were a sharp sword, purposefully prodding at Chloe's injured pride. She turned her head and pressed a warm kiss against his jaw.

He swallowed. The woman made him feel things he certainly didn't have a right to. Yet.

Arm's folded, Chloe spun away from them, kicking at the pool's stone wall.

Case considered that they might have pushed her too far. Now was probably the time to turn the tables. He released Kyra and reached out to touch Chloe's arm. "You can come too, if you want." He tried to sound like he was torn between the two of them.

And right on cue, Kyra gave a jealous little sound that was half huff half snort. "Case! I came all this way to spend time with you. Does she have to come?" She sidled up to him and danced one finger down his chest, pouting up into his face.

Case resumed their former position with her in his arms, his chin on her shoulder. But this time he focused all his charm on Chloe. "The thing is... I think Chloe can maybe get us some really good stuff. Isn't that right, Chloe?" He winked at her. Pursed his lower lip out just enough to plead without going overboard.

Chloe actually blushed. He hadn't thought a girl as jaded as her still had a blush left in her.

He grinned playfully and rocked Kyra a little. "See, hon? I told you I could hook us up out here."

Kyra jutted her chin with a miffed grunt. "This stuff better be as good as you claim. I could have stayed home and gotten high with Shane on the regular stuff."

Oh, Kyra was good. And he didn't miss the light of realization in Chloe's eyes that this might be just the thing she needed to put a wedge between them.

He released Kyra and spun her to face him. "You been seeing Shane behind my back now that I'm out here?"

Kyra's eyes widened, then narrowed. "And what if I have! At least he's *there* with me!"

Case threw up his hands. "Oh, here we go! It's not like I had a choice about this move, Darcy!"

Kyra suddenly spun toward Chloe, eyes blazing. "No. Maybe you didn't, but what did I find the moment I got off the ferry to surprise you? You! Here at the park! With her!" She flung a sweep of her hand from Chloe's head to her toes.

"Excuse me?!" Chloe glowered.

"Darcy, that's not fair!" Case stepped between the girls and pushed Kyra back a little like he was trying to protect Chloe. "Chloe has been nothing but a friend."

Kyra peered past his shoulder, giving Chloe another glower. "I bet she has!"

"Oh whatever!" Chloe cursed and barreled around him to get right in Kyra's face. "You want some of me, girl? You've got me!"

Whoa! Was this going to come to blows? Case bit back a grin. Kyra looked just as surprised as he was by that challenge. He needed to step in before Kyra got hurt. She was scrambling for a comeback.

Chloe didn't let her get that far. She put up one hand to stop his approach. "For your information little miss goth wannabe, Case has been nothing but loyal to you since he moved here. Sounds like you haven't returned the favor though. You don't deserve him!" She accompanied her last words with a shove to Kyra's chest that was so violent it rocked both of them back from each other.

Pfft! The soft *whap* of a bullet was followed only a moment later by the report of a rifle echoing off the rocks of the fountain, and Chloe collapsed at their feet, blood gushing from her forehead.

For one suspended moment, silence seemed to freeze everyone in the park, and then chaos took over.

"Oh! Dear Jesus!" Kyra's scream held genuine shock and terror.

All around them screams sliced through the morning as families and tourists dove for cover.

"Get down!" Case tackled Kyra and pulled her behind the rock wall of the fountain's pool. He pushed her as close to the wall as he could. "Stay here!" Thankfully, she didn't look like she was going to disobey.

Kyra curled on her side and rocked, hands gripping her hair. "They shot her! They actually shot her and it's all my fault."

His jaw tightened. Not her fault. Not her fault at all. But he didn't have the luxury of time to tell her that right now.

The yoga class must have ended when he wasn't paying attention, because he could see several of the women crouched down and hiding near cars in the parking lot. The picnicking family had all gathered behind the steps that led up to the top of the bright red tube slide. Everyone else who'd been in the park seemed to have vanished from sight, which was good.

He snaked forward until he could see Chloe once more. She was out in the open, but he had to get to her! She could still be alive and if he could drag her here to where the cover was, they might be able to save her. It was a split-second decision, and then he was moving.

He charged forward, grabbed Chloe's ankle and then lunged

back toward the fountain. A bullet spit up dirt near his feet. He grunted and tugged with all his might. Something snatched at his sleeve near his shoulder, and then he was back behind the protective wall of the fountain, once more.

From the corner of his mind he registered that Kyra seemed to have recovered from her momentary descent into shock. She was on the phone and it sounded like she was talking to the 911 operator. Where had her phone been?

He listened even as he set to work assessing Chloe's injuries. The shot to her head wasn't as bad as he'd first feared. The bullet had grazed along the skin of her forehead, and blood was everywhere. He could see the white of bone, but it didn't appear to have penetrated her skull. He blew out a breath of relief.

Kyra said. "Three shots, yes. And one young girl critically wounded."

Case tugged off his sweatshirt and turned it inside out. He pressed the clean side of the material to the gash in Chloe's head. Feeling for her pulse.

There was a pause in Kyra's end of the conversation. "I don't know..." The wide set of her eyes and the paleness of her face told him the question the operator had just asked her.

He tried to offer a reassuring expression. "She's alive. Tell them the bullet just grazed her. But she likely has a fractured skull. Her pulse is fast and light."

Kyra relayed the information. Thanked the operator. And hung up. His earlier fleeting question of where her phone had been was answered when she tucked the iPhone into the top of one of her boots.

She scooted closer to him, peering down at Chloe with a worried frown. "I'm sorry that I lost it there for a second. What can I do to help?"

Keeping the compress against Chloe's forehead, Case reached out to squeeze Kyra's hand. The truth was, she was doing really great for someone who'd never been trained on how to respond to all the adrenaline that pulsed through people in situations like this. But if he could get her to take over with Chloe, he could get to work tracking down the shooter. It would take the police some time to get here, and by that time it might be too late.

"I need to go after the shooter. Do you think you could stay here with Chloe until the paramedics can get to you?"

She nodded, but her gaze was fixed on his left shoulder. "You're bleeding." She reached for him.

He glanced down. Frowned. Blood gushed down his arm, soaking him all the way to his wrist. Yet he wasn't feeling any pain.

Kyra pegged him with a look. "Do you have a pocket knife?"

He nodded. He never went anywhere without one.

"Good. Give it to me." When he complied, she took over holding the compress to Chloe's head while demanding, "Off with your T-shirt. I need to look at that wound. You can't go chasing someone down in your condition. We have to stop the bleeding first!"

Case followed her directions, and then wished he hadn't. The wave of pain hit him like a fifty-foot tidal wave. Another bullet spat chunks of rock off the top of the fountain's base.

They both flinched lower.

Kyra was furiously working with something on his sweatshirt, but she glanced at him worriedly. "Are you okay?"

He wasn't sure. He glanced down at his arm, which was now bare. Thankfully, he could see an exit wound. A bullet must have entered his bicep from the front and exited out the back. He pulled in a breath, willing down the pain and nausea coursing through him.

When Kyra scrambled to his side he realized he'd forgotten to reply.

She assessed the wound. "Never mind, I can see that you're not. Here." She had worked the elastic band from the hem of his sweatshirt free and cut it in half so that it was a long stretchy strip. She tied one knot in it, measured it against the width of his arm and tied another knot, then tied the whole thing around his arm good and tight with both knots pressed to the entrance and exit wounds. She was barely done before she dropped a soft kiss against his shoulder and then belly-crawled back to Chloe. "You're good to go," she said over her shoulder. "Just come back to me, Case."

He was suddenly reluctant to leave her. What if the shooter saw him leave and came around to get a better shot? She might be left vulnerable and alone. He rubbed at his forehead trying to decide what to do, then gritted his teeth when no ready answer came to mind. This was why there was a rule about never getting involved with someone while undercover. It messed with decision making.

His phone chimed and he pulled it from his back pocket. A text from Mick. "Text to Radell came from a burner. But new 911. Come home ASAP." With a grunt of frustration, he shoved it back in his pocket. Mick was just going to have to wait a bit.

In the distance he heard the sound of the approaching sirens. Kyra would have help soon, but no one would be able to get to her and Chloe until the active shooter was cleared from the area. That spurred him forward.

Crouching low, he sprinted for the nearest cover, which was an overturned trash can. Snatching it up, he hissed against the pain and raced for the stone building that housed the park's bathrooms just ahead.

Bullets chased him, but each ended up harmlessly in the dirt. And he was thankful to have them aimed at him. That way he knew the shooter hadn't moved yet.

Once he was behind the building, he tossed the trash can aside.

Anger burgeoned in the place of the shock and adrenaline and pain.

Whoever this shooter was, they were going down. Right now!

The kid disappeared behind the bathrooms and panic suddenly began to set in. From there he could make a straight line up into the woods and come around from behind. There would be no good shots. Besides it was clear that more time at the shooting range was needed.

Is he really coming to find me? Or just trying to escape?

Either way, it was time to go. Even if the kid was just making an escape, the sound of sirens had grown louder now. It was time to get moving. Fingers hurried to dismantle the rifle. Fumbled. Faltered. Floundered.

Calm down!

A breath in. Hold for the count of three. Release. Repeat. Trembling stopped. And disassembling the weapon resumed.

Cop cars screeched to a halt in the parking lot.

Ten seconds. Maybe less before capture was imminent.

Leave it!

But the last two sections were apart now. Shoved into the bag. Bag to shoulder. Walk calmly. Straight down to the park.

A curse burst out. None of this should have been necessary!

A huge cement planter that held a cascading lace-leaf maple, vibrant orange from all the recent cooler weather, provided cover to cower behind. With arms curled over ears in pretense of terror, there was a moment to assess.

At least Chloe had gone down. That was the main concern. It would have been better if a second shot could have been put into her. But Case had grabbed her before the thought had registered.

Had she been speaking to Case and the strange girl long enough to reveal anything damaging? Hopefully, the shot had taken her down before she had said anything incriminating. It had appeared that the two girls were engaged in a jealous squabble, so maybe they'd only been meeting as friends and a fight had broken out over the boy. Maybe Chloe's purpose hadn't been to tell them anything at all.

Hopefully.

And yet hope was no foundation to build a criminal career on.

Teeth clenched tight. *She better not have revealed information!*

No new texts had been sent to Kyra, so that was good. Still, it might be good to go back to her place and take her out just to prevent any of the other kids from talking to her. But then... Another curse. With each need for cleanup came additional risk. Taking her out might reveal more than wanted. Hopefully this action against Chloe would speak loud and clear to the other kids.

Speaking of kids... Who was the goth girl? Had she come over on the ferry? An old girlfriend of Case's maybe? Likely. But none of that was what piqued the curiosity.

Something tugged for attention—rattled at the back of the mind.

The boy's reactions after the first shot... Those weren't the reactions of an untried high school kid, were they? The way he'd tackled goth-girl down behind the fountain. Then risked himself to pull Chloe out of danger. Precise. Quick. Effective. Using cover to his best advantage.

Almost military in movement? Or... A gasp slipped free. A cop?!

Just then stealthy footsteps sounded and a man spoke from just behind. "We think it's safe to move people now. If you'll come with me we'd like to evacuate the park."

All oxygen seemed to vanish upon recognition of the voice. Sheriff Holden Parker.

Muscles tensed so violently that the officer had to have noticed.

Breathe just breathe! Holden doesn't know anything.

Slowly, muscles relaxed. Arms uncurled, hefted the bag, slung it over one shoulder. And then with forced ease and a smile that hopefully looked more normal than it felt, the shooter turned and looked Holden in the face.

His brows shot up. "It's you! Are you alright?"

What was a normal reaction? Trepidation. Definitely shock. The hand visible around the strap of the bag did plenty of shaking anyway. A little added tremor to the fingers used to scoop at a strand of hair added to the picture of a terrified trauma survivor. "Yes, I'm fine."

Holden reached out and took an elbow. Pulled until they were both over the curb and onto the grass. "Did you see anything?"

More trembling, and this time there was no need for theatrics. A shake of the head. "No. Not really. I was sitting on this bench enjoying a cup of coffee"—a convenient detail able to be inserted because of the Java and Juice cup that lay empty on its side on the bench—"and when the shooting started I dove for cover."

Holden gave a sympathetic twist of his lips. "Alright. Well, come this way. We are asking everyone who was in the park today to wait over here by the play structure. But one of the students was injured by a bullet. I may need you to talk to her if you feel up to it? Sometimes kids will reveal something to someone they trust more easily than to a cop."

"Of course. I'm always happy to help." Lips pressed together, the shooter refused to allow the smile of triumph to emerge. Providence, it seemed, was smiling down today.

If Chloe was alive, this was the opportunity to finish her off.

Chapter 15

Kyra prayed for Case like she had never prayed before. And as she knelt over an unconscious Chloe she prayed for her too. Thankfully, there wasn't much she needed to do other than to keep the compress firm against Chloe's forehead, because her hands trembled to the point of near uselessness.

And she wasn't at all sure that it was because she had just been shot at. The trembling had started deep inside the moment Case's lips had touched hers and had magnified tenfold the moment she'd seen that wound in his shoulder.

She knew for Case the kiss had just been part of the cover. But wow! Silken lips framed by the texture of several days of raspy stubble. And despite the fact that they'd been role-playing, she'd appreciated that he had tempered the kiss with gentleness and subtlety. She felt another curl of desire just at the memory! It was a good thing she had been deep in her role as Darcy. Otherwise her knees might have buckled and her reaction would have given away the whole ruse.

And then he'd been shot. And was currently headed into the face of danger to try and stop a would-be killer.

Her trembling grew worse. And she renewed her fervent prayers. *Jesus, just bring him back to me, please? I'll give another try at relationship if You'll please keep him safe! Put guardian angels on every side of him and please stop the bleeding in his arm and don't let there be any lasting effects from that gunshot wound.*

Just thinking the words *gunshot wound* made her feel faint.

Was the shooter the same person who had been doling out drugs to the kids? If so, why had they suddenly switched to such aggression?

Chloe moaned, rolling her head from side to side.

"Chloe!" Relief at having her alive and moving was juxtaposed with the fear that she might do real damage to herself by thrashing around. "Lie still! Just lie still. I've got you." Kyra cupped the girl's cheeks in her hands to keep her head in one place. Like Case had said, the likelihood of a fractured skull was high. Plus, though no more shots had come for several minutes, the shooter could still be out there. If Chloe tried to sit up she could put herself in more danger.

Something at the back of her mind pulled for her attention. Why had Chloe been a target in the first place? She was just a kid!

"What happened?" Chloe's words weren't much more than a rasp. But then her eyes widened and she tried to lift her head even as her hand fumbled to feel the ground close to her. "My phone! Where's my phone?"

"Shhhh!" Kyra tried to reassure her. Crazy teens and their phones. "You were shot, but I think you are going to be fine. I just need you to lie still, okay? Help is on the way."

"My phone." Chloe insisted. "Can't let 'em find it!"

"I don't have your phone, sweetie. It's over where you fell..." Even as she said the words her focus drifted to where Chloe's bright red phone lay clearly visible out on the grass.

The sensation that had earlier whispered for Kyra's attention leapt up and this time demanded that she pay attention. There was something here that she should realize.

"Listen." Chloe clutched at her. "Have to...give it...to...the cops. Tell them...protect...Miss...Radell." She tapped at the sweatshirt still pressed against her wound. "My fault." With that, Chloe slumped once more into unconsciousness.

Cops? Miss Radell? Her fault?

Every thought seemed to be working its way through sludge before it registered. But it was only a moment later that Kyra's heart slammed against her rib cage.

The phone! The texts! Her eyes widened and she returned her focus to the iPhone out on the grass.

Had Chloe been the one who sent her those texts this morning? And if so, had the dealer somehow found out about it? Decided to eliminate Chloe to protect his identity? That would mean that the shooter and the drug dealer were in fact probably the same person! And Chloe knew who they were! She had to get to that phone and she had to tell Case!

Chloe needed to be put under protective custody!

Footsteps drew her attention to their right.

She'd never before been more relieved to see an officer approaching. She tipped her head toward the trees where the shots had been coming from. "Shots were coming from up there." Did the man know about Case? Since she didn't know the answer to that question, she decided to leave him out of it. But wait... What if one of the officers saw him moving and took a shot at him?

"There's a...student headed in that direction. Case Sheridan."

The man gave no indication whether he knew Case was a cop or not. He only nodded. "We have officers on it. I need you to scoot back but stay under cover. I'm going escort these paramedics over there so they can start working on her. Alright?"

"Yes." Kyra happily complied, scooting forward to make more room for the others behind the cover of the low wall.

"The shot grazed her just above her brows. She just woke up a moment ago. I tried to keep her as still as possible."

One of the paramedics spoke into the mic on his shoulder. "Victim is unconscious with massive head trauma. Prep an OR. ETA, fifteen minutes."

Her gaze returned to Chloe's phone. Only a few feet away, but it might as well be across the ocean.

And yet... No shots had been fired for several minutes. Didn't it stand to reason that the shooter would have packed up and run the moment the sirens sounded? Yes. It did. And if Chloe wanted the cops to have the phone, it most likely had evidence on it!

Just go get it.

"I'll be right back," she said to the officer, and then she lurched forward.

"Hey! Come back here!"

Kyra had intended to run all the way to the phone, snatch it up, and return to cover, but the moment she got out in the open it was as though her body refused her command to keep moving. Frozen in a half scrunch, shoulders curled up around her ears, she held her breath. Was she about to be shot?

"You can't go out—" The officer's words fell away when no shots came.

Relief released her and she hurried forward, but Simon Hall was already there, bending down to pick up the phone. He was still wearing his jogging clothes. His backpack was slung over one shoulder. Behind him, Sheriff Holden Parker was also escorting Principal Vaughan, who must have been either coming from or going to a meeting because he had that large satchel briefcase he always carried. A few others who'd been in the park trailed in their wake, and a very shaken Ashley Adams, who also wore exercise clothes and carried a gym bag, leaned on the sheriff's arm.

Kyra's attention returned to the phone. Her mouth went dry at the sight of it in Simon's hand. She remembered Case's words of caution about him.

He inspected it slowly, then lifted his gaze to hers, brows furrowing. "Were you coming for this? Risking your life for a phone?"

She nodded. "It's Chloe's. She was injured. And she wants it." She held out her hand for it, willing away her quavering, but Simon ignored her.

He brushed past her. "Yeah. The sheriff asked the three of us"—his gesture took in Ashley and Principal Vaughan—"to come over. He thought that since Chloe has known all of us for years, our familiar faces might soothe her a bit until her parents can get here."

One of the paramedics barked, "Well she's currently unconscious, so she won't know the difference."

"Terrible tragedy." It wasn't clear if Simon had registered the paramedic's words. "Who would do something like this?"

Principal Vaughan seemed like he might be in shock. His jaw gaped a bit as he took in the surroundings with a bit of vacancy in his eyes.

"Shouldn't one of us ride with her to the hospital?" Ashley asked.

The paramedic was all business, continuing to work as he shook his head. "Can't. Sorry. Only family can ride in the aid car with the victim."

Sheriff Parker patted Ashley's hand where it rested on his arm. "Sorry. I knew you wouldn't be able to be in the car. But I thought if she was conscious when we got over here you three might be able to soothe her."

There was something about the sheriff's words that drew Kyra's attention. Several minutes ago, one of the paramedics had announced over the radio that Chloe was unconscious. Wouldn't the sheriff have heard that?

Another thought hit her. Case had mentioned that both Simon and Ashley were at the top of his suspect list. He'd probably communicated that to the sheriff, right? So was the man just trying to keep an eye on both of them?

She felt a wash of shock. Could Simon or Ashley have been the one doing the shooting?

If the sheriff had suspicions why would he have brought them this close to Chloe, though? Wouldn't he want to keep them as far away from her as possible? And yet...what better place to keep an eye on them than here where they were both close together and surrounded by cops?

And the information on Chloe's phone just might reveal which one of them it was! But the sheriff didn't know that yet.

She scrambled frantically for a plan to get that phone out of Simon's clutches. If he was the dealer and the shooter, and there was incriminating evidence on there he could destroy it. And if he wasn't the killer, having the phone might put him in danger. She didn't want that either. She couldn't picture Ashley trying to harm him, but hadn't Case mentioned that there was someone else who had jumped to the top of his list this morning? Who was that?

She gave her head a little shake. This was all too much to figure out. Her brain was going to turn into a pretzel if she didn't stop thinking so hard. She didn't know who to trust or not to trust, but what she did know was that she needed to get that phone.

Simon paused and spun back to face her. "Who are you? I saw you earlier, didn't I?"

Kyra was taken aback for just a moment until she remembered she was in disguise. She'd been forgetting to alter her voice since the shooting had commenced!

Sudden fear threatened to steal Kyra's ability to speak at all. Her story about arriving with the morning's only ferry would fall all to pieces if Simon mentioned that he'd seen her walking on the community trail. And if someone had recognized her voice? *Get back into character, now!* The less details she gave, the better. She could do this. "I'm Case Sheridan's girlfriend. I live over on the mainland." She eased into the slight accent she'd been using earlier, hoping that the transition wouldn't be noticed. She glanced past him toward Chloe, who the paramedics now had on a rolling stretcher. "Case and I were talking with Chloe when she was shot. Anyhow..." *Be bold!* She strode right up to him. "Like I said, Chloe wants this, so I'll just take it to her so she'll have it in the hospital with her." She grabbed the phone but Simon refused to release it.

"And where's Case now?"

Careful. She waved her free hand toward the trees. "I don't know. He just took off running that way." She rolled her eyes. "Boys! I guess he's no knight in shining armor!"

They both stood there, each of them with one hand on the phone, staring into the other's eyes.

Don't blink.

Something twitched near Simon's left eye. Was he reluctant to give it up to her because he believed she was a stranger? Or because he knew there was incriminating evidence on it?

Sheriff Parker spoke as he brushed past them with Ashley leaning heavily on his arm. "Oh just give her the phone, Simon. The goal here is to make Chloe feel as relaxed as possible. If the girl wants the phone, she gets the phone." In that moment, the sheriff gave her a pointed look, and she suddenly knew that he knew she wasn't any such thing as Case's girlfriend from over on the mainland.

Maintaining her grip on the phone, she arched a brow at him. Would he give it up now? And if not, what would she do?

Simon reluctantly released his hold and Kyra eased out a breath.

Sheriff Parker pegged her with another look as he helped Ashley to a seat on the wall of the fountain near Chloe's stretcher. "I'm going to need to speak with you in just a moment, young lady. I'll need to know everything you saw."

She nodded. "Yes, sir."

The paramedics were now rolling Chloe toward the ambulance in the parking lot, one of them holding a bag of IV liquid high above her.

Realizing Simon, Ashley, Vaughan, and the sheriff were staring from her to the red phone in her hand and back again, Kyra hurried after the stretcher. Of course she couldn't really leave the phone with an unconscious Chloe. She needed to get the device either to Case or to the sheriff. But she needed to make this look good.

While the paramedics loaded Chloe into the unit, she turned her back to the group and bent as though brushing dirt from her knees. It only took a second to shove Chloe's phone into her empty boot and extract her identical phone from the other. Her heart hammered. That had probably looked really suspicious, hadn't it? But a quick glance back at the group near the fountain showed that, though they continued to watch her, none of them seemed suspicious. The paramedics were still locking the stretcher into place, barking orders at each other, and scribbling on tablets. She stood waiting by the open doors of the aid car.

If she could pull this off, maybe when the sheriff questioned her she would have an opportunity to hand over Chloe's phone to him. Where was Case, anyhow? It worried her that she hadn't seen him for several minutes. So much adrenaline was coursing through her that she almost dropped her phone. Finally, the last paramedic started to climb on board.

Kyra held up the red phone, making sure that it was plainly visible. "Could you give this to her when she comes around?"

The paramedic dropped the phone into a plastic bag and scribbled something on the outside. "I'll be sure to get this to her. I'm sure she'll appreciate it."

Kyra nodded. "Thank you." As casually as she could she turned and walked back toward the group near the fountain.

The deed was done. Mission accomplished. She had Chloe's phone.

Next step. Get it to the police.

Anger seethed. So close to boiling over.

The phone had been right there. But that goth girl had won the battle.

On top of that, the snippy paramedic had prevented anyone from accompanying Chloe, and it wasn't like a scene could be made in front of all the lawmen on the island.

Something coiled tight deep inside. This whole thing could come unraveled at any moment.

What was it about that goth girl that seemed so familiar? Something niggled at the back of the mind, but couldn't quite be pinned down.

Well, whatever it was, it didn't really matter. The phone had been returned to Chloe. And thankfully she was unconscious still, which meant she wouldn't be talking yet. So it would just be a matter of retrieving the phone from the hospital now, and a plan was already forming for how to do that.

What did Chloe have on that phone? The thing was... She might have nothing on it, but the risk couldn't be taken. This was a situation where the potential benefits far outweighed the dangers.

Stand up. Casually pick up the bag. Don't forget to act

traumatized. "Well, I don't know about you all, but I think I'm ready to get out of the park for today." A little nervous laugh. "I'll just run over to the hospital to wait for the Schumachers to arrive. Make sure Chloe's alright until then."

It was a good thing Holden had been a friend for so many years, or he might have wanted to search the bag. Even as it was, the slight suspicion in his expression hadn't been too hard to decipher.

Even now the sheriff's gaze dipped to the bag. But all he said was, "It was a blessing that things weren't worse here today. I'll swing by your place later this evening to ask a few questions if that's alright?"

Panic nearly took over. Holden couldn't go poking around at the house. He might find the supplies in the spare room. And that would be bad. Very bad. "I'm not feeling much like cooking. I think after I leave the hospital, I'm going to eat out in town and then go to bed a little early. This"—a sweeping gesture encompassed the park—"has kind of worn me out. Mind catching me at The Rusty Bucket in a bit? That will save you a trip out to my place anyhow. I know it's not that far, but looks like you are going to have your hands full this evening. Still, you have to eat, so burgers are on me."

Holden's clap to the shoulder was firm and friendly. "Of course. I understand and yeah, that sounds good. Give me forty-five minutes to clear things up here."

A nod. A smile that hopefully looked weary around the edges and not simply nervous. "Sure thing. That will give me time to sit with the Schumachers for a while."

Now walk.

Holden exchanged a few indecipherable words with his deputies as the parking lot grew nearer.

The car was just ahead. The bag slung casually over one shoulder felt like it might be flashing a neon sign. But escape was just one click of the key fob away. The trunk popped open and the bag disappeared into its depths. The trunk clicked shut. Driver's door opened. Soft leather seats welcomed and enveloped a body that was now trembling beyond control.

Just drive out of the parking lot then you can pull over and get yourself together.

Thankfully, there was push-button start because at this point the quaking likely would have prevented the key from finding the key hole.

The engine purred to life and the gearshift slid easily into drive.

It wasn't until the exit from the park had been reached that a glance in the rearview mirror revealed that the kid Case had returned to the group by the fountain. He and the goth girl—had she ever even said her name?—were exchanging an embrace.

Lips pursed. Hmmm. Maybe the girl really was the kid's girlfriend from across the water. And maybe he really was nothing more than a high school kid who'd performed a heroic rescue of Chloe and then taken off out of terror for his life.

Right. And I'm British royalty.

No. No indeed. There was definitely something off about those two. Couldn't figure it out just yet. The cop angle was probably right on which was bad. Very bad. If the kid was a cop that meant he was here to investigate Fire. And that presented a whole new problem. A problem that sent a cold fury coursing through already icy veins.

What should I do? Not panic, that's what. Deep breath in. Slowly ease it out.

The answer would come. The mind was a curious thing. Often when one quit trying to figure out an answer to a problem, *poof*, the answer just appeared.

And right now there were more urgent fish to fry.

Get rid of the gun.

Fetch Chloe's phone.

Have dinner with the sheriff.

Maybe get some sleep. All this deception really was wearying.

And somewhere in there the answer to what was off would reveal itself. Because it always did. Always.

Chapter 16

Kyra had never been more relieved to see someone than she was to see Case striding toward them from the direction of the hillside. She wanted nothing more than to break into a run and enfold him in an embrace but managed to keep her feet rooted sturdily to the grass. He was on the job. The last thing he needed was a flighty female throwing herself at him, no matter how relieved she was to see he was still alive.

But even as she was thinking those thoughts, Case reached out and tugged her into a one-armed hug. He looked down at her and winked. "Better if we keep up pretenses. You okay?"

She nodded and settled against his side, curving one arm behind him and resting the other against his stomach as she searched his face. Had he seen anything? Found the shooter? She quirked one brow hoping he would be able to understand her question.

He gave a subtle shake of his head.

Kyra tried not to be so shallow as to notice the enticing feel of his taut stomach muscles beneath her hand and failed miserably. And it ought to be illegal for a man to wear whatever scent that was—spice and sport and ocean breezes all wrapped into one. Guilt washed over her. He'd been shot doing his job and all she could think about was how attracted she was to him. "I should be the one asking if you're alright. We need to get you to the hospital to get that shoulder looked at. But first..." Though they'd been speaking so softly she felt certain none of the others could hear, she wanted to be doubly cautious now. She stood on her tiptoes on the pretense of pressing a kiss to his cheek, and whispered, "I have Chloe's phone. She seemed very insistent that I get it to the police. But I wasn't sure who we could trust." She gave a pointed lift to her brows and a subtle tilt of her head toward the officers and people by the fountain.

Case glanced over her shoulder and gave her a small nod of understanding.

Kyra continued to whisper. "Case, I think Chloe might have been the one who texted me this morning."

He nodded and drew her closer, still portraying the image of a couple in love. "Yeah, I wondered the same thing even before I got here. Where's her phone at?" He asked the words with his mouth pressed to her ear and one hand cupping the back of her head as he swayed with her gently.

Kyra closed her eyes, doing her best to concentrate. She certainly hoped they looked like a couple who was merely concerned about each other after a traumatic event, because as muddled as her thought processes were right now, her acting skills were likely severely lacking. That realization made her blush. To Case this was probably all just part of the job.

When he pulled back and looked at her, she realized that she hadn't answered him yet and hurried to say. "In my boot."

His lips thinned into a smile of understanding. "Okay. Keep it hidden until we can get alone with Holden." He ran a thumb over her cheek, looking deep into her eyes. "When this is over I certainly hope you'll reconsider your answer to that question I asked you at your sister's salon that first day."

Kyra's heart stuttered and she searched his face. Did that mean what she thought it meant? "M-maybe I could be coerced into rethinking my answer."

Case chuckled. Then winced. "Yeah, maybe it's time for me to visit the hospital now."

Kyra nodded. "Is your car here? I can drive you."

"Young man, I'd like to ask you some questions." Holden was suddenly standing right next to them.

And just like that Case morphed back into a teen boy. "Sure." But from the exchanged look that passed between them, Kyra knew that they were assessing each other as one cop to another. Case made a quick hand gesture before he spoke again. "Do you mind if we do this at the hospital though? Because I'm in some royal pain right now."

Holden's eyes settled on his shoulder and widened. "Yeah. Not a problem. I'll swing by your room once they get you checked in."

Case frowned. "I'm hoping that won't be necessary."

Holden scanned his arm once more. "It will be. I'm betting surgery is in your future."

Case lowered his voice further. "You know that can't happen, man."

Kyra felt her heart go out to him. He'd poured so much of himself into this case. But surgery for an undercover agent in a small community like this would mean his cover was blown wide open. Surgery would require a medical history. And for Case to give them that, he would have to reveal who he really was. News like that would spread like wildfire in a community this size.

Sheriff Parker leaned closer. "I have some news. We just heard from Deputy Saunders who stayed at the precinct to field calls when people started phoning in about this shooting. Candice Vaughan showed up just a few minutes ago. I'm going to talk to her now and will let you know what she says."

Kyra figured this was just as good a time to interrupt as

any. She held out her hand. "Keys. Come on. We can talk about that later. For now, let's just see what the doctor says."

Holden's eyes darted to Kyra and she could tell he was wondering if she was another cop.

Case offered a begrudging twist of his lips and lowered his voice further. "Holden, I believe you know the new teacher in town Kyra Radell?"

Holden's eyes widened as he took her in from head to toe. "You brought her in on this?"

"She sort of brought herself in," Case mumbled. With a gentle glower in her direction, he plopped his keys into her palm. "Anyhow, she has some evidence that we hope is going to give us all the information we need. Meet us at the hospital? Too many eyes around to hand it to you right now."

Holden nodded. "I'll be there as soon as I can."

Chloe's phone hadn't been hard to get to at all. The life-long friend of the shocked and grieving family—someone everyone in the community knew and trusted—hadn't even been questioned after telling the nursing staff that Chloe's parents needed her phone so they could contact her friends and let them know she'd been hurt.

Her parents waited in the small hospital's only waiting room and would get the phone in just a few minutes. But not until it had been examined and deleted of all incriminating evidence. The same story would be given to them. Didn't they think it was a good idea to rally a support team around Chloe? Maybe calling the friends on her phone would help them pass the time until the surgeon could come out and give them all an update? It would be spoken with soft tenderness and the most caring expression. And no one would even question why the phone had been entrusted to a non-family member.

Hurrying. Breaths coming a bit too fast. But a glance back toward the hospital proved that no one was even paying attention to the fact that the phone hadn't been carried immediately to the waiting room.

Locks chirped open and a loud breath of relief puffed free as the pine scented interior of the sedan welcomed once more.

Everything could have gone so wrong today, but it hadn't. The only concern that remained was over Chloe. If she lived through the surgery, something might have to be done about her. No. Something would have to be done about her. She could still talk. And that couldn't be permitted.

But for now...

The iPhone was cool against the lips pressed against it in gratitude. "Let's see what you've been up to, Chloe dear."

Encrypted. Of course it was. But that wasn't going to be a problem. The glove compartment opened with a gentle tug, and the small tablet inside weighed hardly anything more than the phone itself.

A few taps on the device brought up the run screen for the decryption program. Plugging the phone into the tablet and hitting the run button on the screen set off a series of code that went to work on the phone.

It was only a moment later that the screen of the phone unlocked and offered access to everything inside.

"That's my girl." A gentle pat to the tablet expressed pleasure with the decryption program that had taken a mere five years to perfect. Not even Father would be unimpressed by that if he could be here at this moment. Pride surged. Sometimes it was such fun to be a genius.

Now...what to check first. "Pictures. Always the pictures."

One tap opened up the gallery, but immediately concern raised its head. What was this? Pictures of a woman and a couple kids were the main focus of the photos—unfamiliar people. But there was an ugly little dog, and—a gasp escaped—some selfies.

A string of curses filled the interior of the sedan as anger hot and volatile boiled up inside.

"That's why she looked so familiar!" Fists pounded the steering wheel. That stupid goth girl from the park hadn't been a stranger at all! It was Kyra Radell. And this was her phone!

They must have the same phone! You've been played for an idiot!

That meant that Kyra had Chloe's phone right now, this very minute!

"You senseless moron!" She'd made the switch right in front of all of them and no one had noticed! *At least I didn't.*

Panic covered brow and upper lip with a sheath of sweat and it was suddenly much too hot in this blasted car!

Think! Would she have given the phone to the cops yet? Had she had time? Wait! Was she a cop herself? Undercover as a teacher? Partnering with the new kid too?

Head dropped against headrest. "Oh, you are so dumb! How did you not see that!?"

Always the failure. Just like Father predicted.

Teeth ground against each other.

No! Once more, this was *not* going to be the destiny that won out. There was still time! Something could still be done. It was just a matter of figuring out what to do.

The phone tap-tapped-tapped against pursed lips, as plan after plan zipped across the mind's eye. No. No. No. Each plan was rejected before it could even be fully thought through. All of them required exposure. Too much exposure.

And yet... This was life or death here. Happiness, wealth, and freedom, weighed against spending the rest of life behind bars, or worse. If ever there was a time for a bit of risk, this was it.

I need...

And just like that, the answer presented itself. For there, pulling into the parking lot, was Kyra driving Case's car. He was in the passenger seat looking a bit peaked.

A smile bloomed. Chest released its tightness.

Once again, destiny smiled down.

The plan fell into place. A plan that required hardly any risk whatsoever if everything went as expected. Yes! Yes. This could work.

Kyra helped Case from the car and supported him as she escorted him into the ER entrance.

Toss the iPhone and tablet into the glove compartment. Take up the keys. Feel them cool against a sweating palm. Breathe. Just breathe.

Everything was soon going to be set right again.

Everything.

Kyra was worried. More worried than she let on. Case's arm was still bleeding badly and he hadn't said a word since they'd left the park. Thankfully, the hospital was on this end of town and it had only taken them a few minutes to get here.

Her relief couldn't be quantified as they entered into the ER and a nurse spotted them and rushed forward, tugging a gurney behind her. "Hey there. What's going on today?"

Kyra helped Case ease down onto the rolling bed. "He was shot. At the park. About thirty minutes ago."

The nurse *tsk*ed. "Heard there might be a second victim joining us." She was already busily working over Case, assessing his arm, feeling for a pulse in his wrist. "Are you family?" She flicked a glance in Kyra's direction.

Kyra shook her head.

The nurse focused on Case. "Are you coherent? I'm going to need you to answer some health history questions."

His lips tilted up into that maddeningly calm smile of his. "As coherent as ever. My name's Chris Pratt and this is the year 2033."

The nurse blinked at him.

He grinned. "Don't worry. I know it's not 2033 yet."

The woman angled Kyra a glance. "I think we're going to have our hands full with this one."

Kyra knew she should smile and play along, but all she could seem to do was stare at the man's mangled shoulder.

"Hey." Case reached out with his good hand and squeezed her arm. "Don't worry about me, I'm going to be fine. Don't look so glum. I'm the one who feels like someone tried to saw my arm off." He ended that statement with a wink. But when she didn't respond in kind he pressed the issue. "Kyra, I'm going to be fine. It's not my dominant arm, so it's not even going to hold me back much from work. Don't worry."

She tried to offer him a smile. She really did appreciate his attempts to make her feel better, even if he wasn't doing that good of a job.

The nurse turned and swept Kyra with a searching glance. "Were you injured at all?"

Kyra shook her head.

"Then we'll take it from here." And with that she wheeled Case through a set of swinging doors and disappeared from sight.

"She can come with me." Kyra heard Case protest.

But the nurse dismissed him with, "Sorry. Family only. She can come..." The words trailed away, too indistinguishable through the batwing doors to be deciphered.

Kyra wrapped her arms around herself and studied her surroundings. Did she just go home? Or should she wait here?

She didn't really have any reason to stay. Case was in good hands now and would be taken care of. Except... She *wanted* to stay.

To her left a good-sized waiting room held several couches and tables covered in magazines. A TV up in the corner played some college football game between two teams she didn't recognize. A family huddled in one corner, a woman dabbing at tears and whispering tortured phrases to a silent, slumped man beside her. His elbows were on his knees and his hands hung limply. If he leaned any further forward, he might topple from his chair.

Kyra recognized them as Chloe's parents from that night at the Harbor House. They looked so in need of some support that she'd started toward them before she even thought better of it. "Mr. and Mrs. Schumacher?"

They both lifted their gazes to hers, but neither seemed to truly see her.

Kyra stretched out a hand. "I'm—" She paused. She had almost introduced herself as "Kyra Rydell, Chloe's teacher from the high school," but remembered her disguise just in time. She switched to "I'm Chloe's friend, well, really a friend of a friend from the high school. Would it be alright if I sat with you for a while?"

"Of course." The mother tried to smile through her tears. "I don't think we know you, dear?"

Chloe's father had returned to staring at the space between his knees. His lips were moving and Kyra suddenly realized that he was fervently praying.

Realizing Chloe's mom was still waiting for her reply, Kyra offered a sympathetic smile. "My name is Darcy." She felt bad for lying to these people when all they wanted to do was grieve and hope and pray for their daughter, but she reminded herself that Case's life could be in danger if she did anything else.

"Mildred! I was so sorry to hear about Chloe!"

Startled, Kyra twisted in her chair to see Ashley Adams hurrying across the waiting area, arms outstretched. Both Simon and Principal Vaughan followed on her heels.

Ashley leaned down and wrapped Chloe's mom in a warm embrace. "I was as the park doing yoga. It was just awful. Is she going to be okay? What did the doctors say?"

Mildred Schumacher shook her head and dabbed at her eyes again. "They didn't—don't—know what to expect. She was unconscious when they took her into surgery. They figured her brain was probably swelling. "How could something like this happen? In our little town! We've already had so much tragedy. I'm just—" She dropped a hand onto her husband's knee. "We're just, so shocked. Oh, there's Holden too." Mildred stood and pulled each of the three men into her embrace. "Holden, thank you for responding to the situation at the park so quickly. What happened? Do you know yet?"

Holden looked grim. His glance flicked off Kyra's. He shook his head. "We are still investigating. I wish I had more to offer you. We'll let you know just as soon as we know anything that we can say, alright?"

"I understand." Mildred put her Kleenex to use again. "It's all just so baffling. Our Chloe is a good girl. I just can't..." Her voice broke and she sank back into her seat giving in to sobs.

Mr. Schumacher came out of his stupor long enough to reach an arm around her and tug her close and then, with his wife crying on his shoulder, he went back to staring into space, lips once more moving.

Simon, Vaughan, and Ashley sank wearily into nearby chairs, but Holden remained on his feet. He glanced at her. "How was Case doing when you got him here?"

"As good as could be expected, I guess. He was halfway teasing the nurse when she took him back into the ER."

Holden nodded. "Good." He shuffled his feet. "I think everyone here could probably use a cup of coffee, but I won't have enough hands to bring them all back. Can I talk you into coming down to the coffee stand with me?"

Kyra's heart gave a little leap of relief. This would be perfect. She could give the sheriff Chloe's phone and they could get to figuring out what was on it that the girl had been so concerned about. "Of course. I'd be happy to."

She stood.

Holden smiled. "Thanks. The coffee shop is in the main lobby on the other side of the hospital, but I know a short cut." He glanced to the group seated around Mildred and her husband. "What can we bring back for you all?"

After taking everyone's orders, Kyra followed Holden across the room and into a narrow hallway.

He led her past a taped-off construction zone cluttered with tools, pipes, and boards of varying lengths. It appeared the hospital was doing some work on the bathrooms in this section of the building.

As they walked, Kyra studied the man. He was a broad-shouldered hulk of a guy with blond mussy hair that on a less handsome man would have just appeared unkempt, but on him gave off a rakish vibe that only increased his good looks. In fact, if she wasn't already interested in one Case Lexington she would—

That thought threw her. What was she going to do if Case didn't make it? No matter his teasing attitude, with as much blood as he'd lost his situation had to be really serious. She'd found him handsome from that first day in the salon, but handsome wasn't everything. And yet since that time he'd proven to be a man of courage and honesty. Someone who would sacrifice himself on behalf of total strangers to make the world a little better place. And his sense of humor and concern for her didn't hurt any either.

Kyra bit her lip. *Jesus, please bring him through the surgery and protect us all from this crazy person.*

Holden pushed open a swinging door to a perpendicular corridor and allowed her to enter before him. As soon as they were inside, he reached out and pulled her to a stop. "We can get coffee in a minute, but I really asked you to come with me so you could give me Chloe's phone." Holden propped his hands on his hips and peered down into her face. "Are you really the new teacher from the school?" He shook his head and waved a hand. "Never mind. Do you still have it? Based on some other things that happened this morning I think we have this drug dealer nailed. But I'm hoping the phone will have the evidence I need to convince a judge to give us a rush warrant."

Kyra started to reach toward her boot. "Who do you think it—?"

The door behind them exploded open. There was a loud, hollow *clunk*. Holden's eyes went glassy. He fell in a crumpled heap at her feet.

Heartbeat thundering, and confusion swirling through her, Kyra stared down at him, jaw agape. The humming, flickering, florescent lights of the narrow hallway revealed an ooze of blood pooling beneath Holden's head and seeping along the tiles.

A metal pipe clanged against the floor, bouncing and rolling until it came to rest in the corner.

Kyra lifted her eyes and her focus seemed to freeze on the barrel of the pistol pointed right at her chest.

"I want Chloe's phone and I want it now."

Chapter 17

Case dropped his head against the hospital bed pillow. He was grumpier than a cat whose milk had just been taken away.

The moment he'd started giving his real name and social security information to the hospital staff, he'd seen looks being exchanged and whispers being passed. Mick had shown up, flashed his credentials and informed the doctor that he was to do everything in his power to save his officer. Case's cover was blown, but that was the least of his worries.

He'd allowed Kyra to put herself in harm's way. He should have sent her packing the moment he'd realized it was her in that crazy disguise. Thankfully, she hadn't been hurt. The thing was, now that things were heating up and he'd realized that Chloe's texts were what had set off this whole firestorm, he didn't want her to leave his side. And yet the doctors had told him that he was going to need surgery, immediately. It was scheduled for three hours from now.

But his main frustration didn't stem from any of that. No. It was over the fact that he hadn't caught the drug dealer yet.

Out there somewhere right now, a low-life kid killer was gloating, thrilled to have gotten away with yet another escapade. Only this time he'd seen that he could use a gun in a public area and still escape squeaky clean. Case's hand fisted around the blankets.

"Stop it."

Case opened his eyes to see that Mick had stepped into his

room. He stood near the door, hands thrust into his slack's pockets. "I can see that you are beating yourself up over this. None of us could have known that this dealer was going to escalate to a shooter. Besides this op blew wide open today. I've been trying to get a hold of you. Didn't you get my texts?"

Case scraped his good hand back through his hair. "I was a little busy getting shot and trying to catch a shooter. What happened?"

"Yeah, true. Sorry. Anyhow, Mr. and Mrs. Vaughan are separated, did you know that?"

Curious over where this could be going, Case nodded. "I just figured it out this morning. She came to the school to talk to me, apparently at Vaughan's request, but then got a text and rushed off."

"Well, they just recently separated and before she came to the school she stopped by their house to get a few more of her things. She noticed some suspicious stuff. She didn't want to get Vaughan in trouble if her fears turned out to be unfounded, but there were some bags of orange crystals. She found them on his kitchen counter."

Case's heart gave a leap. "No way. Vaughan? I had him pegged for innocent."

Mick sighed. "Believe it. She had a chemist friend of hers from college who lives on the island test some of it. And when it came back with the ingredients it did, she rushed immediately to the precinct, and when his deputy heard what she had to say he called me as well as Parker."

Case felt a wash of cold fear. "Vaughan was at the park! He's the one who tried to kill Chloe?"

Mick frowned and rubbed the back of his neck. "Yeah, we think so. Parker mentioned he seemed really shaken, but he just thought that was from being shot at. Any idea why he would shoot Chloe?"

Case's mind scrambled to orient all the events of the morning. "Yes. I think I do know. And that means—" Another wave of terror rammed through him. "Kyra has Chloe's phone! Vaughan is going to want that. We need to get to it first. Can you go down to the lobby and get Kyra? She's dressed like a goth with a dog-collar thing around her neck."

Mick's brow scrunched. "Dog collar? What in the world?"

"It's a long story." Case was too terrified for her safety to explain it all right now. "Can you just go get her? I'm fairly certain some texts a student—we think it was Chloe Schumacher—sent to her are what set this whole thing off. You should probably post a guard on Chloe too. I don't like this, Mick. I really don't like this at all."

"Alright. Alright." Mick held out a soothing hand. "I'm on it. I'll have her up here in just a few minutes. And I'll put a guard on the kid. Damian is headed this way on the ferry as we speak. I called him the minute I heard from the deputy. So he can help out through the night. You just lay back and relax." He started for the door, but froze. "What the—"

Holden Parker stumbled into the room, holding the back of his head. He leaned heavily against the wall.

A nurse rushed in on his heels.

"Holden, you really need to come with me—"

"Just give me a second." Holden brushed her to one side. "Someone knocked me out from behind and when I came to, Kyra was missing. Worse than that, she didn't have time to give me the phone. So Vaughan has both Kyra and the evidence!"

Case was already pulling the IV line from his arm before the man had even finished his sentence.

"Hey, you can't do that!" the nurse chastised.

"Watch me." He thrust his legs into the pants they'd only moments earlier made him take off, shoved his bare feet into his shoes, and snatched up his shirt, gritting his teeth against the pain. "Let's go." He pushed Holden's shoulder to urge him out the door. "Show me where you were when you were knocked out."

Heart hammered as Holden's body crumpled to the floor and Kyra's wide eyes registered recognition. She would have to die now, but every war had casualties. *Hold the gun steady. You are the one in charge.* "I said, I want Chloe's phone and I want it now."

Repeating the command didn't seem to get through to Cedar Harbor High School's newest teacher, however. She remained frozen with her hands up near her ears. "I don't know what you are talking about." Her voice was barely audible and gruff with fear.

Patience wearing thin, the next words snapped out. "Don't give me that! I know you and Holden concocted this coffee run so you could give him Chloe's phone. Her *real* phone. Because the phone that you so innocently handed to the paramedics at the park, was *yours*, Kyra Radell."

That earned a satisfying blink. Her hands even shook a little.

There was no time for this! "Come on! Where is it? Hand it over!"

Kyra's mind seemed to be scrambling. That much could be told from the way her gaze kept darting down to Holden and then back up again.

"Stop thinking. Stalling won't do you any good. Just give me the phone."

Kyra moistened her lips, but still said nothing.

"Listen, you've got about three seconds to comply or I'm going to have to knock you out and search you for it."

Kyra's eyes narrowed just the slightest bit. But it was

enough to raise caution. Caution that morphed into full out fear when she said, "I have a black belt in karate."

There was no real threat to the words, and yet they made every hair on the arm holding the pistol stand on end because sudden realization washed from head to toes. Kyra's hands were not held up by her ears in fear, but in an attack ready pose! It was suddenly very clear that proceeding with the utmost caution was probably the best course of action.

You didn't plan on that *did you?* Father's voice mocked from the back of the mind. Teeth slammed together. This had been planned so perfectly. All of it! Right down to the little detail of planting evidence at Principal Vaughan's house where Candice was sure to find it—well okay, maybe that little detail had fallen into the lap, as it were.

This morning at the gas station. They'd both been pumping gas, and Candice had been on her phone like she was nearly all the time. It had seemed like pure providence to overhear her say she was running back to her apartment for the house keys she'd forgotten, and then she was going to go pick up a few things from the house while Vaughan was at the school supervising detention. She'd offered the detail that she didn't like to get things from the house while he was there because there was "too much tension."

It hadn't taken more than a few minutes to drive over to Vaughan's house, pick the back lock, plant the baggies of Fire on the kitchen counter, and then make an escape.

Honestly though... Maybe Candice loved her man more than the separation indicated, because she hadn't run right to the cops. If she had, Vaughan would have been arrested for immediate questioning, but he'd been wandering around the park like the traumatized survivor he was, just a bit ago. And the way the cops had treated him made it very clear he wasn't high on their suspect list. At least not at that point.

At their feet, Holden moaned and started to stir, drawing the mind back to the present.

A quick jab with the pistol indicated the exterior exit down the hall. "Move!"

Thankfully, Kyra didn't try any of her black belt moves—if she really even was a karate expert.She seemed happy to do as she was told, for the moment. Did she really know nothing about the phone? Could one of the paramedics have made the switch? But how would they have had Kyra's phone? No! It *had* to be her. She was just stalling for time! Well her time was running out, and fast!

As Case and Mick hurried to follow Holden down the hospital hallway, the nurse rushed after them. "Did you say you are looking for Principal Vaughan?"

All three men froze and spun to look at her.

"Yes." They spoke in unison.

"Well, I just saw him in the hospital lounge not more than two minutes ago. I had just passed through there and was cutting down that back hall when I saw you"—she gestured to Holden—"stumbling for the stairs and followed you up here. Vaughan was sitting with the Schumachers."

Holden was already speaking into the mic on his shoulder, but Case didn't wait to hear his instructions. He also wasn't bothering with waiting for an elevator. He pushed into the stairwell and took the stairs two at a time, Mick fast on his heels, and Holden right on their heels.

"My officers are on their way now." Holden's footsteps thundered down the stairs behind them.

Case had the fleeting realization that they must present quite a sight when they all three burst from the stairwell door into the hospital waiting room. "There!" he pointed.

Vaughan was sitting on the near side of a cluster of seats with the Schumachers, just as the nurse had said.

"Virgil Vaughan, you are under arrest!" Holden's gun was already out of its holster and leveled at the startled man's chest.

"What in the world..." Vaughan's hands shot into the air.

Mr. and Mrs. Schumacher looked just as startled by the proclamation. "Holden, what is this about?" the pastor asked.

"Get down on your knees." Case motioned Vaughan toward the floor.

The principal only stared at him dumbly.

"These are both undercover officers, brought in on my request to help me figure out this drug situation. The gig is up, Vaughan." Holden moved a little closer, making the threat of his gun more imminent. "Candice found the drugs at your place this morning. We were only waiting for a warrant."

Case was done waiting. He pointed for Vaughan to take note of the pistol that Mick now held on him too. One of the drawbacks of being undercover in a school was the no firearms requirement, but thankfully Mick was under no such restrictions. Case looked Vaughan right in the eye. "Don't make me tell you again, to get on the floor. What have you done with Kyra?"

The man sank to his knees in front of his chair, hands thrust in the air. "Drugs at my house? And Kyra? Do you mean Miss Radell? I have no idea what you are talking about!"

A sudden queasy feeling lodged in the pit of Case's stomach. He glanced around at the group, even as he accepted the handcuffs Holden passed to him and cinched them around Vaughan's wrists. "Holden was just knocked in the back of the head a few minutes ago, and when he woke up Kyra was missing. How long has Vaughan been here?"

Pastor Schumacher sputtered a little. "Why, Vaughan got

here about the same time as you, Sheriff. He hasn't left our group since before you went to get us coffee."

The bottom dropped out of Case's stomach. He glanced around the circle of people. Vaughan was there of course. And the Schumachers. Ashley Adams hadn't moved from her chair this whole time, her wide eyes indicated her shock at all that was transpiring. The only one missing was—

Mrs. Schumacher dabbed at tears beneath her eyes. "Simon said he was going to go help you all bring back the coffee. But we haven't seen him since he left."

Case released his hold on Vaughan. "Parker, give me a gun. His car was in the hospital lot when Kyra and I pulled in!"

The cold frame of Holden's ankle pistol was little comfort in his grasp when he rushed out into the parking lot and Simon's green Corvette was gone. He loosed a word he rarely used, and then was immediately convicted. He tossed a glance toward the sky. *Forgive me. Please protect her.*

Case pinned Parker with a look. "Any idea where he would go?"

Parker squeezed the back of his neck. "His property is out in the woods a ways. He mostly keeps to himself. But I think he has a shed on the back side of his acreage. Either his house, or the shed. Those are the only places I can think of."

Kyra's mind scrambled as Simon prodded her away from the hospital at the point of the gun. The ferry whistle sounded. Another ferry was arriving already? Had it truly been that long since she'd melded in with the tourists this morning? But other than that sound, the hospital parking lot lay silent and still.

Despair threatened to steal even the strength to breathe.

They'd reached his car now. "Stop!"

She complied, feeling the bite of his pistol grinding into her spine. Leaning around her, he opened the driver's door. "Get in. Climb all the way across. And don't try anything or I *will* shoot you."

It took her a moment to crawl past the gearshift. Tempted as she was to lash out with her heels, the thought of that pistol held her in check. Once she was settled into the passenger side, Simon sank into the driver's seat. Still holding the pistol on her, he leaned over and thrust his hand into the closest boot. When he didn't find Chloe's phone there, he repeated the process with the other boot. Satisfaction curled his lips when his hand emerged with Chloe's phone.

Ahead of them a nurse parked and got out of her car. Her turquoise scrubs and purposeful stride were all business.

Kyra opened her mouth to scream, but the point of the pistol slammed into her temple.

"Not a sound," Simon ground out.

Kyra quailed as the woman disappeared inside and Simon pulled from his parking space. With the Corvette's darkly tinted windows, there was no hope of someone from outside being able to see her now.

"Reach into the back and grab that blanket." Simon demanded.

Hands weak with terror, she complied, finding a thin, fuzzy, camouflaged lap quilt. She held it out to him.

But he shook his head. "Put it over your head. And keep your hands where I can see them."

They drove for about twenty minutes. Periodically, he jammed the gun into her side to remind her not to try anything stupid.

Willing away her terror, she bided her time, praying the whole way that Case would miss her and come looking for her. But the comforting sound of sirens hadn't yet cut through the morning. The car decelerated. Turned onto a gravel road by the sounds of chattering pebbles beneath the tires. A few minutes later the sound slowed, and the car came to a halt.

No rescue seemed likely at this point. Tears stung her eyes.

There was a whoosh of air, a pause, and then the passenger door yanked open and Simon took her by one arm, hauling her out. The blanket fell away, but he didn't seem to care about that now.

She glanced around, squinting at the brightness of the sunlight streaming through the swaying branches of towering evergreens. His Corvette was parked in the curved gravel drive in front of a log cabin. Weeds choked two flowerbeds on either side of the short walk that led up to a porch, but Simon didn't take her that direction. Instead, he pushed her around the side of the house and onto a wooded trail, heaped up here and there by the roots of the evergreens. She stumbled and fell, pebbles and pinecones cutting into her bare knees.

He cursed her, no longer bothering to temper the volume of his voice, and yanked her painfully to her feet by one arm.

The fact that he wasn't even bothering to be quiet any more made realization dawn. No one was coming for her! Her knees threatened to give out and take her to the ground again, but this time for good. *Jesus!* It was the only prayer she had the strength to utter, but it was enough.

Calm slowly seeped through her. The quaking deep inside, settled.

There was no more time to wait! If she didn't act, her life was going to be over before anyone could help her.

She hadn't lied about being a black belt. There were a lot of kicks she could try, but the roundhouse would give her the best chance at actually knocking him out.

The only problem was, she'd never tried a roundhouse wearing stiletto heels before. Nor had she ever been faced with the threat of a gun, though they'd talked about that plenty in class. She'd also never attempted one while her victim was this close. *Okay, make that problems.* But she was willing to risk all the drawbacks. A little space, however, was key.

If she could just put some room between them...

She tossed a glance over her shoulder. His face was a mask of stone. Nothing of the kind school teacher that she'd thought him to be remained.

"Move!" He shoved her again.

Kyra picked up her pace. "You're never going to get away with this." Her false bravado didn't fill her with reassurance. She knew it was a lie. Worse, she knew *he* knew it was a lie. She cast another glance to assess the position of his body.

He only smirked. "I already have. But you know that already." His gaze swept over her, anticipation lighting his eyes. "I hope you're not afraid of fire?" His smirk turned to a laugh that shot her through with terror.

Did he mean Fire the drug? Like he planned to force her to OD? Or fire fire? Like he planned to burn her to death?

The thought of either option made her mouth dry with horror. Metallic fear coated her tongue. Her vision turned blurry around the edges.

"Where are you taking me?" Maybe if she could get him talking he would remember his humanity and release her. At the very least it might help her hold onto her sanity.

"Shut up!" He shoved her forward again, this time into a little clearing before a shed.

Just the amount of separation she needed!

She balanced on the balls of her feet. Flexed forward as though she was still stumbling. In a flash, she tucked her shoulders, twisted her hips, and spun into a back-roundhouse kick.

At the same moment car doors slammed from back down the trail!

Kyra wasn't sure if she pulled the kick because of the sound, or if Simon flinched toward the sound on impulse. Whatever happened, her kick only ended up glancing off his shoulder.

He cursed her, dropping his backpack as he rushed them forward. "Get in there," his voice was once again quiet but demanding.

Still off balance from her missed kick, Kyra didn't have the footing to fight him, and in the blink of an eye, she was shoved inside the shed and the door clicked shut behind her. Darkness descended.

Something heavy clunked into place. Kyra's heart fell as she recognized the sound as a heavy wooden board being dropped into brackets. She'd just been barred inside.

Something skittered across the floor just ahead and to her right. A shiver of revulsion slipped down her spine. She scrunched her eyes tight, willing them to acclimate to the darkness so she could see if there were any tools in here that she might use to help herself escape.

And then she realized that Simon no longer had a gun trained on her. "I'm here!" she yelled, as loudly as she could. "In the shed! Help!" She was pulling in another breath, planning to scream at the top of her lungs when the sharp scent of gasoline froze her in place.

No!

She heard the distinct crackling of the blaze and saw the angry orange glow clawing through the back corner of the shed almost at the same instant. The ancient ultra-dry wood was almost melting beneath the hungry march of the fuel-spurred fire.

Scream!

Her inhale turned into a smoke-choked cough that only grew worse with each breath.

Stumbling back, she slammed her shoulder into the door.

It only flexed a little, then rejected her. She tried again, still to no avail. Tears streamed from her stinging eyes now.

Flickering tongues of fire had now devoured the entire back wall of the shed and started to make their way along the beams of the ceiling.

Could she leap through it?

With the dim illumination she could see that the back of the shed had been stacked to the ceiling with old wooden crates, all of which were now in various stages of burning. She was in an old, spiderweb-infested, gardening shed. But there were no tools. Just a rickety wooden shelf to her right, and an old wooden wheelbarrow to her left, and the conflagration of crates at the back. No way to leap through those flames. Nothing to help cut her way out. No other exits but the boarded-up door behind her.

Kyra's eyes fell closed.

Realization took her to her knees.

She was going to die.

Burned to death in this garden shed.

And she was never going to see Case again.

Chapter 18

Case's heart slammed against his ribcage at the sight of the Corvette, doors wide open, and idling empty in front of the cabin. Already gone! Where to? He searched the area frantically.

A cloud of smoke boiled like a thick black pillar into the sky behind the house. "This way!" He tore around the corner of the log cabin, with the others hot on his heels.

The trail was only faintly visible, through the wide-open spaces between the thick trunks of the immense trees, but the thick layer of pine needles had been disturbed by recent footsteps. His breaths pounded against his teeth. He barreled forward.

"Case! Slow down!" Mick called from behind him.

Vaguely, he realized he was moving too fast for safety, but this was Kyra they were talking about! He had to get to her!

"Come on, partner! Let's work together on this!" Damian's voice was firm. Case was glad that he'd arrived on the ferry and shown up at the hospital just as they were all piling in the police cruisers to come out here, but he didn't let the man's caution slow him down this time.

The sound of a faint cry came from the glowing and crackling shed now visible ahead through the trunks of the trees.

God please!

It was too far. The flames were moving too fast. He wasn't going to get there in time!

With his eyes on the cabin, he didn't see a mounded-up root. He sprawled flat out. Skidded a ways before a pine tree brought him up short. Agony shot through his shoulder. Radiated clean to his toes. But he'd already scrambled to his feet. Lurched forward.

Damien grabbed his arm and hauled him back. "You can't go closer!"

"I have—"

Just then the back wall of the shed gave way. Sparks shot up, glowing orange against the darkness of the green branches overhead.

Case lurched to a halt and propped his hands on his knees. "No. God, no!" The prayer came too late.

He had failed.

Damian squeezed his shoulder. "Sorry man. I'm cutting wide around back to see if we can pin this guy in. He has to be out here somewhere."

But as Damian melted away into the trees, Case couldn't bring himself to care whether they caught Simon or not.

His whole world had just gone up in flames.

Kyra rested on her knees for only a moment before she clenched her teeth and forced herself to stand. She hadn't taken all those karate lessons learning how to kick for no reason! The shed was old and the wood rotting. Chances were that the brackets holding the door closed might be rotted enough to break free, right?

She backed as close to the flames as she dared, then barreled forward and dove hard into a full-frontal kick.

She heard a splinter, but the doors didn't give. Everything

in her begged for just one full sweet breath of air, but she knew that if she gave in to the urge the smoke would take her down. She might never be able to get to her feet again.

Another run, another kick, another splinter, this one louder. The doors spread wide enough that she could see light on the other side! Hope!

One more time, Kyra!

Backing up again, she put every last ounce of her effort into the run and the kick and this time the doors gave way. She tumbled out onto the ground in front of the shed, coughing and gasping for breath.

"Kyra!"

Case's voice. Relief sapped her of the strength to do anything but breathe.

Then a thought registered. Where was Simon?

She pushed against the ground, oxygen-deprived muscles quavering with the effort. "Case?" the word was barely a rasp. She must get to Case. He would protect her.

"Kyra, I'm coming!"

She stood, swiping at her eyes, trying to see through billowing smoke and tears. One step forward. Then two. She leaned heavily against a tree, glanced up—right into the face of a scowling Simon Hall.

A whimper escaped and she pushed off, but before she could take more than half a step an arm snaked around her neck and yanked her back. "No you don't." Simon's words ground against her ear. "I must confess I'm impressed with your will to live though. Too bad all your efforts were for nothing."

And then, with her clutched tightly to his chest and his pistol pressed firmly to her temple, he stepped out into the clearing before the cabin. "Nobody come any closer!"

Kyra clutched at the arm he angled across her throat and met Case's ice green gaze boring steadily into hers above the barrel of a pistol as he hurried toward them. He gave her the barest hint of a nod before he turned his attention to the man holding her captive. "Give it up, Hall. All the cards are on the table now."

To Kyra's surprise, Simon only laughed. "Oh man, I *was* right. You are a cop! I figured you for a cop after the way you reacted at the park." Simon's feet shuffled backward a few steps, dragging her with him. Behind them the cabin crackled and popped. "I see I winged you. Does it hurt?"

A muscle in Case's jaw bunched and only in that moment did Kyra notice that he was holding the pistol one-handed, with his other arm curled in tight against his torso. He must be in a world of pain right now. But his voice remained steady when he said, "Let the lady go, Simon. This is over."

"Oh no!" Simon stroked her cheek with the point of the gun.

Terror all too familiar returned with full force. Kyra realized that this scenario wasn't going to end well for her. She tried to twist her face away.

Simon grabbed her chin with one meaty palm and forced her to be still. "This isn't over till I say it's over."

Kyra caught a flash of movement from a few trees farther back. Case's boss angled out to one side, while Sheriff Holden Parker angled in the other direction, but both stayed well back from where Case stood. Both men also had guns trained on them. They were sneaking from tree to tree trying to flank him.

"Everybody stop!" Simon demanded, loud enough that they could hear him over the roar of the fire. "Or I take her head off!"

Kyra swallowed.

All the men froze in place.

"You shoot her, Simon, and we take you out in the next

instant, you understand?" Case's voice sounded like gravel under tires.

Kyra felt a tremor shiver through Simon, but at the same time his hold on her tightened. "We just all need to be calm and think this through."

Case nodded. "That's right. We do. And if you think it through you'll realize that you have no way out of this situation, and hurting the lady is only going to make things worse for you."

Simon backed up a few more steps. Kyra could feel the heat of the blaze warming the backs of her arms. Simon muttered to himself now in an agitated fashion. Kyra couldn't make out any of his words, but it was clear that he was processing his options of what to do next.

A billow of smoke, thick and black, drifted in front of them, and when it cleared Mick had a phone to his ear. His lips moved, but he was speaking too low for her to hear his words above all the noise.

Simon must have suddenly realized he was on the phone too, because he jolted. "Hey! No phone calls! Who are you talking to?"

Mick lifted his hands, calmly. His phone still tucked in his right palm. "We've got a lot of people wondering what's going on out here, Simon. I was just explaining the situation to one of the detectives. Trying to keep everyone in their right minds, you hear?"

Kyra saw Case's gaze flicker. Had there been some sort of code in what Mick said?

She felt another tremor sweep through Simon.

Case took a couple steps closer and off to his left.

Simon angled to keep Case directly in front of them.

Kyra was so hot now that she could feel sweat drenching her.

"What do you want, Simon? There has to be something

you want. Just tell us and we'll see what we can do for you." Case took a couple more steps.

Simon gritted a laugh and turned with him. "You think I'm stupid?"

In the background, Mick and Holden started to ease out to the sides again.

"Hey! I told you two not to move! Stay where I can see you!"

Both men froze, hands lifted.

Parker's voice was calm and soothing when he yelled across the distance. "We've known each other a long time, Simon, right? How long has it been?"

Kyra returned her focus to Case and blinked. While her attention, and presumably Simon's, had been on the men in the background, Case had moved a couple steps nearer. And now his gaze was piercing right into hers. His eyes narrowed slightly and his chin dipped a notch at the same moment that she noted the fingers on his injured hand waggling.

She glanced down. He had two fingers protruding. And he obviously wanted her to take note of that fact.

"What are you doing Case? You are about to get the pretty lady here shot! Step back." For the briefest of seconds, Simon pulled the gun away from her head and thrust it toward Case.

Case stilled and his attention returned to Simon's face. "I'm not moving, Simon. Just calm down. See? I'm right here."

The gun pressed to her temple again, and Kyra's eyes fell closed in despair. She was about to get shot. And with that realization came one other. Her only regret was that she didn't have more time to get to know Case. She opened her eyes, sought his out. He was looking at her again, but there was an intensity about his look that made it clear he was waiting for her to understand something.

Kyra fought through the panic, and heat, and terror that

was making every thought ungraspable, trying to figure out what Case was attempting to tell her. And then in a flash it came to her. *Two.* The count was always two. No matter what number he said to Simon, something would happen on two. But...her panic increased. What was *she* supposed to do on two? Just stand there? And what was his plan?

"Simon this is your last warning. Let the woman go and turn yourself over peacefully. Do it now. I won't say it again." There was a deadly calm about Case's instructions that Kyra had never heard in his tone before.

Kyra felt Simon shake his head. "No way, man. Ain't happening!"

Case's eyes suddenly widened. "Kyra, are you with me?!" His brows shot up. "Simon, I'm telling you man, she's about to faint. I've seen this before. I'd say we have about five seconds before she goes limp in your arms!"

Comprehension dawned. Relief nearly made her faint right there on the spot. But she had to wait for two seconds.

Case took two quick steps toward them.

"Shut-up!" Simon extended the gun to stop Case's forward progress. "Kyra don't you dare faint."

Too bad for him, she'd reached the count of two in her head, because she followed orders and slumped into a "faint."

Shots rang out.

Simon's arm around her neck went limp.

Something bounced against the pine needles by her head.

And then she was scrambling. Cowering. Crawling.

She didn't know or care what direction she headed, only that it was away.

Someone grabbed her!

"No!" She fought and kicked. Clawed at a root and dragged herself forward. Swung her elbow.

"Kyra, it's me!"

The heel of her hand connected with flesh and a grunt sounded near her ear.

"It's me, Kyra. You're safe. Everything's over."

Case! The words penetrated her consciousness. The person trying to grab her was Case!

With a sob, she turned and flung her arms around his neck.

He grunted again. And hissed as her weight forced them against a tree. But one arm curled around her and pulled her tight.

Kyra was sobbing then, crying against his neck. "Thank you. Thank you. I was so scared." A root dug into her hip and she scooted closer, further into the safety of his embrace.

"I know you were. But I've got you now. It's all over." His hand soothed the length of her spine but there was something strangled about the words that broke through to her.

"Your shoulder! I'm so sorry!" She jolted back.

All around them was chaos. Several policemen had descended on Simon's body. A man she didn't recognize leaned over Simon and touched his throat, feeling for a pulse, but even as she watched, he shook his head. One of Parker's officers unfolded a large blanket and draped it over the body.

Kyra shuddered. "Oh dear Jesus." Her hand flew to her mouth and she was thankful to already be sitting because her legs felt no stronger than cooked spaghetti. A cough wracked through her.

"Kyra, we need to get up. Get you to the hospital."

"I've got her." A strange, yet somehow familiar voice spoke from beside them, even as the man scooped her into his arms.

Kyra was too startled to resist. Her arms wrapped around the man's neck on instinct. It was the man who'd been leaning over Simon only a moment ago. Handsome chiseled features, and eyes the color of caramel corn, accompanied the familiar voice.

"Yeah. Yeah." Case groused, struggling to his feet. "Just don't get used to carrying her. Because as soon as my arm is better, that's going to be my job."

Kyra bounced a frown between Case and the new man.

Case smiled at her, but it was a bit pinched around the edges. "Kyra, I'd like you to meet my partner, Damian Packard."

Right. "But how did you—"

Case led the way up the trail away from the still snapping fire and chaotic chatter of the officers.

"I was already on my way here. Because you see, my partner here can never quite finish an op without me." Pack offered her a grin.

Case snorted.

They rounded the corner of the house. Red and blue lights strobed from almost every direction. An ambulance sat at the end of the drive and the paramedics descended on them, then, urging Case into a wheelchair, and instructing Damian to carry her to the back of the ambulance so she could be checked out. Over Damian's shoulder she saw Case being loaded into a cruiser that left immediately, lights still flashing.

Concern tugged at her brow. What if he didn't make it because he'd come to save her?

"Hey." Damien jostled her slightly. "Don't worry. He'll be fine. They just want him in surgery sooner than later."

He eased her onto the back stoop of the ambulance, and paramedics bustled to snap an oxygen mask over her face, take her blood pressure, check her pupils. She was being taken care of. Safe. But Kyra couldn't relax.

All the way to the hospital, she couldn't stop coughing, and every breath sounded like it was being sucked through a kazoo. The x-ray was torture because she had to hold still, and they had to repeat the process twice when she coughed at the wrong moment. Her head felt like it might explode while at the same time nausea churned. Through the shower they made her take to clean the grit and smoke off, and into the room where they propped her up in a bed with every machine known to man strapped to her, she worried and fretted and trembled. They took her blood and rushed it down for emergency tests.

Her pulse was too fast, they said. Her breathing too shallow.

For several hours, doctors and nurses flitted in and out of her room with worried expressions and low voiced murmurs of concern.

Kyra tried to calm herself. She tried not to fight the oxygen mask they put on her. But nothing was comfortable, and everything felt out of sorts.

And then Case walked into her room. His arm was wrapped from shoulder to wrist in so many layers of bandages that he looked like the Michelin Man, but his gaze was laser focused on her. And the moment she laid eyes on him, it was as though all was right with her world.

The beeping on the machine next to her slowed from a rapid tattoo to a steady rhythm.

The nurse that Case pushed past to get to her side, smiled and tapped the oxygen indicator on her meter with a satisfied smile. "I guess broken heart really is a syndrome," she chuckled. "I'll be right outside." She pulled the door almost shut as she stepped out into the hall.

Case sank onto the edge of her bed and leaned forward to sweep a strand of hair away from her forehead. "Hey. They tell me you are really going through it."

She couldn't speak past the oxygen mask, but she managed to shake her head. She was fine now. She fumbled one hand across the blankets until she could wrap his good hand in her own. And then her eyes slipped shut.

Case had made it. Until this moment, she hadn't realized

that all her concern and anxiety was over him. But he had made it. And Simon wouldn't be selling drugs to any more of her students In her book, that made for a pretty good end to a pretty terrible day.

With a soft sigh, she gave in to the tug of much-needed sleep, but not before she curled her fingers through Case's, good and tight.

Epilogue

September had stretched into an unseasonably warm October, and overhead gulls soared on warm breezes, calling out to each other. The surf pulsed against the shore, and two little boys giggled from the playground just a few feet away.

Legs outstretched before her, Kyra leaned back against her hands and curled her fingers into the warmth of the grass.

Case lay perpendicular to her, his head resting just above her knee. His arm was still in a sling, but he no longer needed any bandages. His surgery had gone even better than expected and he was slated to regain full use of his arm after several weeks of physical therapy. He angled his face and looked up at her. "You doing okay?"

She transferred all her weight to one hand and allowed the other to stroke through his hair. "Any day spent with you is a good day."

He sat up, scooted a little closer and then propped his good hand on one side of her. "You just seem a little quiet today. Your lungs okay?"

"My lungs are fine." And they were. With lots of rest and a round of antibiotics, she'd made a full recovery from her smoke inhalation scare. "Chloe came back to school today, and I guess that has me thinking through everything again."

"How is she?"

Kyra absently traced a finger down the strap of Case's sling. "She's doing really well considering what would have happened if she hadn't pushed me at the exact moment that she did. Her scar is pretty wicked, but she's scheduled for plastic surgery on that in a couple weeks. And I think this near-death experience really shook her up. I even heard her talking to one of her friends before class about how God has used this in her life."

Case captured her fingers in his own, toying with her first finger. "That's really good. I'm glad to hear it. I always saw potential in her."

"Mmmm." Kyra knew she shouldn't be so gloomy. But she was dreading tomorrow. For the past three weeks Case had been under doctor-ordered rest. He'd spent the whole time on the island and they'd spent every spare moment they could with each other. But all that was coming to an end. Tomorrow he was leaving to go back to work, even if it was only desk duty. He would be across the water.

"That's not everything, is it?" He tilted her a look that urged her to be honest.

Kyra blinked hard. "I'm just going to miss you when you leave."

"Hey now, none of that." Case stroked a thumb beneath her lashes, swiping her tears away. A mischievous tilt tugged at his lips. "You have no idea how happy I am to hear that you're going to miss me."

She frowned at him, dashing at her wet cheeks and inwardly admonishing herself to get her emotions under control. "Why does that make you happy?"

"In your eyes I've gone from would-be serial killer, to delinquent, to a man you are going to miss. I've come a long way." He winked and leaned in to brush her lips with a soft kiss.

The thought brought an unexpected giggle. She was going to miss him, yes. But that didn't mean their relationship had to come to an end. Look how far they'd come in such a short time. She rested one palm over his heart. "You should have seen your face that first day in the salon. You thought for sure you had me and then"—she tapped one finger against his chest—"I shut you down."

He chuckled. "You sure did. And when I walked into your class that first day I couldn't have been more surprised."

"You were surprised! Oh man, I about fell over! I thought I was going to get fired before I even started. Which reminds me that Principal Vaughan told me to thank you for the part you played in getting his wife to give him a second chance. She moved back in with him a few days ago. I guess thinking the worst of him and then finding out he really was innocent all along reminded her of his good qualities."

"Happy to hear it. Maybe I should go around arresting random people who are having relationship difficulties." He winked.

Kyra stretched a gesture across the sky. "It's a bird. It's a plane. It's superman!"

"And don't you forget it." He tapped her on her nose.

She took hold of his finger and pressed a kiss to it. "Never."

Case's smile lingered for only a moment before a more serious expression took over his features. He stroked her cheek with his thumb. "I'm actually kind of glad you were in disguise that day that Simon took you hostage. Because when I think back to it I remember the goth girl and not you with that pistol pressed to your temple."

Kyra shivered. She wished she had the same luxury. "Did they finally finish clearing and cataloging all the paraphernalia that was at his house?"

Case nodded. "Yeah. Hard to believe the massive amount of supplies and equipment that he'd managed to gather. I guess he had some of it shipped to the school, picked some of it up on the mainland, and had other stuff shipped to his house. All in small quantities. I'm really glad we caught him before he started producing that stuff en masse."

"Me too." Kyra turned so that her back was to Case's chest and tugged his arms around her. "Any clues at the house about why he did this? I'm still shocked that he tried to burn me, but not the proof that was found plainly in his house."

"I don't think he had time to get back to the house because we'd already arrived. Either that or maybe he thought he'd gotten away with it. Got too confident?" She felt Case's chin come to rest on her head. His voice rumbled softly when he spoke. "We did find a journal where he raved a lot about his dad. But other than that... Why does anyone evil choose to go that way when others choose to do what's right? I'm not sure I know."

Kyra sighed. "Me either. I'm glad we serve a God who is bigger than all our problems and who understands the human mind better than any of us ever will."

"Yeah, me too." Case gave her a little shake. "Alright, enough gloom and doom. We have to plan our next date. Where do you want to go?"

"Date?" Kyra teased. "I never agreed to go on a date with you. You might be a serial killer."

With a good-natured growl, Case dug his fingers into her ribs and his mouth into the crook of her neck.

She giggled, and started to wriggle out of his grasp, but the thought of his shoulder stopped her. "Hey that's not fair! You know I can't move without hurting you!"

His lips worked across the side of her neck, sending a delightful shiver through her. "What's not fair, is how beautiful you are, do you know that? What's not fair is making me fall in love with you when you live way out here on this island and I'll only be able to see you on the weekends."

Kyra's heart thudded as though trying to escape her chest. "Love me?" The words squeaked out on the barest of whispers. She pushed to her knees and turned until she could look him in the eyes.

Eyes that were all seriousness now. "Yeah, for sure."

Kyra leaned forward, suddenly needing to be so much closer to him. She draped her arms around his neck and pressed the tip of her nose to his. "I love you too."

With a pump of his brows, Case's lips descended to capture hers. "I do believe I've arrested your heart, Miss Kyra Radell."

Kyra sighed happily and gave in to the giggle and the tempting softness of his lips. "Yes, I believe you have, Detective Case Lexington."

"You know I aim to make sure you serve a life-long sentence?"

She smiled against his lips. "As long as you're my jailer, I'll happily do my time, officer."

He hummed a thoughtful note. "Well, alright then. I think we can make this work." With a wink, he swooped back in for more kisses, and Kyra released a happy sigh.

Was it getting hot out here in the sun? Or was that just her heart on fire?

Also available...

You may read an excerpt on the next page...

Chapter 1

Salem Finn propped her elbows on the foyer desk and leaned her head into her palms. She was tired. Actually, tired didn't even come close. Exhausted. Bone weary. Drained. Add all those words together and multiply them by a factor of one thousand and it might land somewhere in the vicinity of how she was feeling.

She only hoped that in her exhaustion she wouldn't make some mistake while caring for Gran. If only her job with D.I.M.E.S. had worked out. The job that would have allowed her to pay for Gran to be in a top-rated care facility. Working for them had been her dream job. But they obviously didn't feel the same about her since they'd quit calling her after the third interview she'd had with them. Gran could be getting the best medical attention possible. Instead, she was stuck living with Salem as her caretaker, and Salem was stuck hoping and praying that nothing too medically challenging ever happened to Gran. Salem also felt guilty about the fact that she was having to leave Gran on her own in her room more than she would have liked. Remodeling and trying to get a bed and breakfast business started took up a lot of time...and energy.

She closed her eyes but immediately snapped them open again. A few more seconds with them shut and her night's guest would find her drooling on her invoices. Then she'd be resigned to greeting him with a crick in her neck to rival Big Bend.

Thankfully, Gran had fallen asleep without too much fuss tonight, though Salem was still half expecting to hear her bedside bell ring followed by a plaintive request for another cup of chamomile tea, or to have her pillows readjusted, or a cramp in her leg massaged out. But last Salem had checked, Gran had been sleeping soundly—much to her relief.

Salem lifted the cup from beside her paperwork, and took what she hoped would be a rejuvenating swallow of the tepid coffee. She needed to power through these bills before her very first, and one-and-only, boarder arrived for the night.

One-and-only.

Her stomach knotted into an ache. The problem wasn't necessarily in powering through the bills, it was in deciding which one she should pay, and which ones she might get away with putting off for a bit.

When she'd taken over her grandmother's care and decided that her best option was to turn the place into a bed and breakfast, which would allow her to generate an income and still remain near Gran all day, she hadn't realized just how much work she would need to put into the place to get it going.

Neither had she realized how much work Gran would be, to be honest. Her grandmother was nothing if not set in her ways. Thankfully, Salem had now renovated and decorated one of the rooms. But having only one room ready for guests was putting a severe crimp in the budget for these first few months.

Still, it was no small miracle that the one room had booked up immediately after she'd posted the availability online. Even if it was for only one night. She would take it.

With a sigh, Salem flipped through the stack of bills. Water. Power. Sewer. All those went in the "need to be paid now" pile. The cable bill she tossed into a separate pile, along with the bill for the internet provider. Though...she studied those last two, tapping her fingers against them...guests might get upset if they arrived and had no wifi or cable options in their room. With a little groan, she moved cable and internet to the "must be paid" pile. That left her cell phone bill, which she used as the number for customers to make reservations, so it really *had* to be paid—she plopped it into the appropriate stack—and the waste management bill. That last one she put in its own little pile. If she put off paying that one for a while, she could maybe store the full garbage bags at the far end of the shed and then haul them to the dump later in the spring.

She swiped her phone to life, opened her banking app, and checked her balance. She slipped one hand to the back of her neck and squeezed. If she took the payment her upcoming guest paid tonight, she might have enough to get three of the bills paid. If only the man had wanted to stay more than one night. She might have to do some research on which service provider gave the most amount of grace if a bill wasn't paid on time. The thought sent another curl of apprehension through her stomach.

Jesus, I could really use a little help here? I'm just trying to do the right thing and take care of Gran, but getting this bed and breakfast off the ground is taking more time than I anticipated. And I don't know how long I can do both on my own.

Jett Hudson slowed for a curve in the mountain road, rolling his shoulders and willing himself to relax. He'd been keeping an eye on his rearview mirror ever since he'd left the airport, and it didn't appear that anyone had followed him. Now it was dark and all he could see were headlights. A few cars were travelling the road behind him, but this was only a two lane highway with few places to turn off until they got to the other side of the mountains, so it didn't mean he had a tail.

Maybe his stocking cap, tugged low over his brow, and the several days worth of scruff he'd let grow had kept him from being recognized, as he'd hoped. Or maybe it was the fact that he was a quarterback from Florida landing in Seattle. Or maybe he was just as much of a "has been" as he feared, and no one even cared about him anymore.

He jutted his jaw to one side. Since when had he started to care what other people thought about him? He'd never gone into the NFL because he wanted fame or fortune, though both had come. He'd simply followed his heart and worked hard to be able to keep playing a game he loved. He'd done his best to honor God with the talents he'd been given, and he'd fought to keep his privacy because he wasn't a guy who enjoyed the spotlight. In fact, 'loathed' was a much better word to describe how he felt about the constant scrutiny, both from the media and from the fans. But he'd put up with it all because of his love of the game.

Then he'd taken that hit…

His leg ached, and he reached down to rub his shin.

Once again, he heard the crowd noise. The grunt of the onrushing lineman. The unnaturally loud snap of both his tibia and his fibula. The guttural, instinctive cry of shock he'd emitted as his leg collapsed from under him. The gasp and then horrified silence that had fallen over the home crowd in the stadium. He felt the jolt of the ground rushing up to meet him, and then the jagged shards of pain zipping along the nerves from his leg. His thoughts rushed to the end of that fateful day, to the hospital room where he'd first heard those life-changing words "career-ending-injury." The six months since then had been a haze of surgeries, painful rehab, and the difficult task of resigning himself to his new reality.

He grunted and slapped the power button for the radio. He cranked it up high and willed the country ballad to wipe his memory clean. Old Blue, the truck he'd purchased with cash at the first car dealership the cabby had taken him to, might be ancient, but she had a first rate sound system. Yet, even with the loud tunes pounding through the cab, the memories refused to be banished.

Jett scrubbed one hand over his face.

This trip was supposed to be a time to get away from everything. A time to forget about the past and start looking to the future. What did he do with his life now? He had no idea.

After seven years in the NFL, with stats to rival those of the greats like Aaron Rogers and Russell Wilson, he hadn't even been close to thinking about retirement yet. It didn't matter that seven years practically made him an old man in a sport where the average career lasted about three and a half.

His five-year plan hadn't included metal pins holding his leg together.

With Carrie Underwood crooning in the background, he rounded a bend and the town of Riversong stretched out before him. In the dark he couldn't see much, but from what he'd read of the place, it was a tourist town that attracted a lot of visitors during the winter months for the Christmas festivals and tree lightings the town put on, but remained fairly quiet the rest of the year. Since he didn't plan to be around till Christmas, and since this was just about as far from Florida and fans who might recognize him as he could get, he was just fine with that. He hoped he'd be able to spend a few quiet weeks soaking in some relaxation, maybe a few hikes. Some kayaking. Some fishing. But as he always did, he'd only booked one night to start with. That way if he hated the place, he could move on with nothing holding him here.

He glanced at his phone's GPS. The road he needed was just ahead. He turned right. About three miles down, he turned left into the drive of the Riversong Bed and Breakfast. The sign was pitifully small and hard to see. He hoped that wouldn't be an indication of the kind of service he should look forward to. But even if he liked the town and decided to stay, he could always move to a different place if needed. One night wouldn't kill him.

He parked in the designated area, cut the engine, and stepped from the cab. Rushing water hummed an undercurrent that was accompanied by crickets and a lone bullfrog.

A breath eased from him. Yes. This town might be just what the doctor had quite literally ordered. "Take a break from all the media madness. Get away from all the pressure to make a decision about the future. Relax. Try to just accept what happened. That's an important first step."

Accept.

It was hard not to accept when his leg still pained him with almost every step.

Slinging his guitar over his shoulder, he popped the top on his truck's lock box and pulled out his backpack and suitcase. He locked both the box and the truck and then made his way to the front door of the log cabin inn. A sign painted on an old chalk board held aloft by a large carved grizzly bear proclaimed that he should come on in, so he turned the handle and stepped into the foyer.

Off to his left, he could see a well-appointed kitchen, and just ahead stood a large L-shaped reception desk. A small chrome bell sat on the marble. "Ring it for service" was printed on the placard next to it. Since there wasn't a soul in sight, he stepped toward it, but soft snoring froze him mid-reach.

He peered over the top of the chest-height counter. Sure enough. A woman with long blond hair had crossed her arms beneath her head and fallen fast asleep on the desk. On second thought, she was so small, maybe she was just a girl. Another soft snore slipped from her.

Jett pursed his lips and glanced around. The town might be just what the doctor ordered, but he doubted he'd be staying more than the one night at this B&B. The welcome had been less than exuberant.

He glanced back at the woman. He hated to disturb her, but he hadn't slept for nearly twenty hours, and he was ready for some shut-eye. There didn't appear to be anyone else around, so it was either wake her or sleep on the couch he could see just ahead in the great room.

He frowned.

Rubbed the back of his neck.

Considered how good a hot shower sounded about now.

"Excuse me, miss?"

Find out more about this series here: http://www.lynnettebonner.com/books/contemporary-romance/the-riversong-series/

About Author Lynnette Bonner

A former missionary kid who grew up on the sunny savannah and attended boarding school at Rift Valley Academy in Kenya, Lynnette currently writes from her home in the pacific northwest. You can find out more about her and her books on her website at: www.lynnettebonner.com.

If you enjoyed *Fire* and would like to read more romantic suspense from Lynnette you can find *The Unrelenting Tide* here: http://www.lynnettebonner.com/books/contemporary-romance/islands-of-intrigue-series/

Also, if you would like, connect with Lynnette on Facebook here: http://www.facebook.com/authorlynnettebonner.

Made in the USA
Middletown, DE
18 June 2025